Enjoy
Carol Farris

Two *Kids* Three *Dollars* AND Four *suitcases*

CAROL FARRIS

WestBow Press books may be ordered through booksellers or by contacting:

WestBow Press
A Division of Thomas Nelson & Zondervan
1663 Liberty Drive
Bloomington, IN 47403
www.westbowpress.com
844-714-3454

ISBN: 978-1-6642-0817-9 (sc)
ISBN: 978-1-6642-0819-3 (hc)
ISBN: 978-1-6642-0818-6 (e)

Library of Congress Control Number: 2020919461

Print information available on the last page.

WestBow Press rev. date: 10/28/2020

Chapter 1

Willow Rossi waited on the steps outside of work for her husband to pick her up.

"Happy Birthday again, Willow. Do you need a ride home?" asked John, a co-worker, as he left the building. "We all enjoyed sharing your birthday cake today."

"Thank you, but no, I don't need a ride. Frank is picking me up. He dropped me off this morning so we would have only one car tonight. We're celebrating my birthday at the Bears Den tonight. A few friends are joining us."

"Okay, have fun tonight. See you tomorrow. Happy Birthday again!"

With that John gave a final wave, got into his car and drove away.

In one motion, she waved good-bye to John and turned to see Francesco pull into the parking lot. Willow's eyes danced and her smile stretched from ear to ear as she got into the car with her husband.

"Hi honey!" She was excited to get the evening started and continue to celebrate her birthday. Frank had never been one to make a big deal about gift giving occasions so she was thankful for friends who would help her celebrate.

Willow had been in California for two years now. She met Francesco in a neighborhood pub a few months earlier. The girls she worked with often went to that bar after work on Fridays. Right away she spotted Frank with some other fellows. She noticed how handsome Frank was. They spoke briefly, but he didn't give her much attention.

The following Friday night, when the girls went to that same bar, he pulled out all the stops as he charmed and delighted her. With all the time and attention he had showered upon her since that night, she was smitten.

He wanted to be with her or talk to her on the phone every day. It was more attention than she had experienced in any other relationship. She had never felt so loved.

Willow had been raised in a rigid Scandinavian household in South Dakota, where a display of emotion was rarely visible. Her parents never hugged or kissed each other in front of Willow or her sisters. The girls rarely received hugs from their parents. Apparently it hadn't mattered much to her sisters but Willow craved hugs and attention.

"We get along so well, Willow." Frank declared. " I love you! I love being with you. I can't get enough of you. Lets go to Las Vegas and get married---this weekend."

"I love you too Frank, but that's so soon. Let me think about it. I have always assumed my family would be at my wedding. At least my sister, Lindy and her husband, Lyle, have to be there. She's my best friend as well as my sister. They have a farm and a family. I doubt they can just drop everything and travel to Las Vegas this weekend. Let's call them and see when they can make it."

"That's an idea. I'm anxious to meet them. It's clear you and your sister, Linden are very close. But we can send them pictures. I love you. I don't want to wait any longer to marry you. I want to make you mine. They'll be excited when you call to tell them we are already married. You can call them as soon as we get back home."

Willow hadn't known him long but she knew the effect of his deep brown dramatic eyes and the intense look on his face. When he looked directly at her she could feel her brain melting. It reduced her intelligence to mush.

Willow was sure this was what love felt like and she wanted more of it. So they were married. Her family offered their congratulations but she could sense they were less than pleased.

A few months later, Willow awakened on her birthday and dressed in the new outfit she had purchased to wear that day. It was beige herringbone tweed pants and a matching vest with a white satin blouse. The blouse had a loose tie at the neck over a plunging V-neckline. She was tall and slim and the long flared pant legs with her taupe high heels accented her elegant figure and long legs.

She received more compliments than normal at work. Today, more than ever, Willow was strikingly beautiful. But she didn't know it.

They had driven just a couple of blocks when Frank declared, "We won't be able to go to the Bears Den tonight. My hemorrhoids have really been causing me a lot of trouble all day. I need to get home and lie down."

"Oh, no! I know you have trouble with them. Are you sure?"

"I am really suffering, honey! I'm sorry."

"But I was looking forward to spending the night with everyone tonight, Frank." After a few minutes of silence, Willow said, "You have to call the bar and tell them we aren't coming." Her voice cracked.

Frank did not respond as he turned the car toward home instead of in the direction of the bar. Willow stared out the passenger-side window, not wanting him to see her tears. But he could tell by her posture and her muffled sniffles that she was crying.

With his left hand on the wheel, and without a sound, his right hand suddenly swung around and struck her in the face.

He began screaming, "It's hard enough to put up with the pain I'm going through without having you sitting over there crying like a big baby!"

Willow was stunned, shocked and scared. She was confused. *What was that?* she wondered in silence. He had been angry before but he had never struck her.

Her cheek began to sting. His large hand had struck her face hard. When they arrived home, no words were uttered by either of them. Silence ruled all evening as Frank fixed a sandwich for himself.

Willow wasn't hungry.

Willow went into the bathroom to look at her face. Her left cheek was reddening, and she noticed color starting also over her left eye.

Willow hoped the redness would all disappear by morning because tomorrow was Friday, a workday. Frank stretched out on the couch.

After changing into her nightgown she slipped into the sheets. But she didn't sleep except to drift off for a few minutes at a time. Her mind kept her awake as she went over their conversation trying to figure out what she had done or said to cause him to slap her. Later, waking up briefly, she could hear him breathing next to her. He had moved from the couch to their bed at some point.

Not really believing his pain alibi for the tirade, she recognized that it had taken attention completely from her birthday and the fact that he lacked a gift for her. Besides getting no birthday gift she had a rather large bruise on her left cheek.

Willow had been aware for some time that Frank was exceedingly jealous. Still searching for answers, she wondered if it was possible he feared she would be getting all the attention? She couldn't believe that he would ruin her birthday simply to satisfy his selfishness and jealousy. *He loves me. I know he does.*

She finally slept. When she was awakened by her alarm Willow got up to shower and get ready for work. She sensed the quiet in their apartment. Frank was already up and gone. The shower stall looked dry so she knew he had skipped a shower. He always showered before leaving for work. *Hmmm. I guess he wanted to get out of here without risking waking me.*

As she passed the large mirror over the bathroom vanity, she caught a glimpse of her face and stopped cold. Her cheek was purple! A deeper color ran up into her eyelid. Frank had likely seen her face as she slept.

Oh! Oh! Oh! I can't cover all that with make-up. There is no way I can go to work today! Wait! It's Friday. I have no appointments scheduled. If I don't show up today, John will think we went out and had too much to drink.

What can I use for an excuse? The flu? Food poisoning? Yes! That's a perfect excuse! I'll call Tina.

"Good morning! Landry's Furniture and Flooring. This is Tina. How may I help you?"

"Good morning Tina, this is Willow. I'm glad you are there early. Listen, something I ate last night didn't agree with me. I must have food poisoning. I've been in the bathroom most of the night. Anyway, let John and everyone know I won't be in today. OK?"

"Sure will, Willow. Sorry you're not feeling well. Hope you feel better soon. Take care of yourself and hopefully we'll see you Monday."

"I will. I'm going back to bed right now. Thanks, Tina."

Hanging up, Willow exhaled an audible sigh of relief.

This will get me through the day. With the weekend ahead hopefully I can cover with make up, what's still on my face by Monday.

Friday was a long day for Willow. She and Frank had not had a conversation since they came home the night before. Surely he would come straight home from work so they could talk.

But he didn't. By six in the evening she knew that he had stopped at the bar rather than driving right home after work.

At seven a cheerful Frank waltzed in the door as if nothing was wrong. He was carrying a brown sack holding two huge burritos and two large Cokes.

"I hope you didn't eat yet, baby cakes." That had been his nickname for her. "I know how much you love these burritos. If you've already eaten, you can put yours in the fridge till tomorrow."

"I'm starving." Willow said. She hadn't given any thought to eating. "Thanks." Willow didn't leave the couch. Frank tossed her a tea towel to put over her crossed legs to catch what might fall out of the giant burrito. He sat in the chair next to the couch using the end of the large coffee table for his burrito.

This particular sidewalk vendor made the best burritos in all of East Los Angeles. They used large amounts of pulled beef, refried beans, peppers, massive amounts of mozzarella cheese, and unknown secret spices. It was a treat Willow truly enjoyed.

Frank quickly absorbed himself with the latest episode of a cop show they both enjoyed. He adeptly charmed her, made her laugh and distracted her. He didn't mention her face and she forgot about it temporarily because, for the moment, she was happy.

This evening had been nicer than any she could remember in the past few weeks. She didn't want to ruin this wonderful atmosphere by bringing up his fit of anger, from the night before.

They went to bed and made passionate glorious love. Willow knew he loved her as much as she loved him. She would have to learn what set him off and not do it anymore.

Saturday morning Willow's face was green. On Sunday it was yellow and brown. Monday morning she knew she had to go to work and raced to her bathroom mirror. There was still some leftover coloring but she knew she could use her skill to camouflage the remaining color, with extra make-up. The eye bruise seemed slower to heal. It would be necessary to use a little more eyeliner than normal, even if it looked tacky. She had to cover the bruise.

Hopefully no one would notice or mention her extra eyeliner or ask her about it.

Chapter

2

After work, Francesco stopped at the bar most days. Willow didn't make evening plans for the two of them because she had no idea what time he'd be home or what his condition would be when he did arrive. She rarely held dinner for him because all too often she had to throw it out.

A few weeks later, he arrived home late, and seemed agitated. Willow made light conversation, hoping to calm him. Bad things happened when he was agitated.

She relayed a story about her younger sister Marigold, who had called that day and was upset with her husband.

"Mari told me she had been bawling all day because she was so upset with Jason."

With that, Frank slapped her with his open hand. Wham!

Willow looked at him in disbelief. "What was that for?"

"You never use that word! You don't even know that word! Who do you know who uses that word?"

His anger was mounting.

"What word are you talking about?" questioned Willow.

"You just said Mari was balling all day. Who have you been hanging around who uses that word?"

"My sister, Marigold said she had been bawling all day, as in CRYING. It was her word," Willow shouted as the tears of fear began to flow.

Frank was embarrassed but refused to show it. He stomped into the kitchen and started making himself dinner.

Willow began to tremble. She didn't want to be alone with him tonight. She quietly slipped out of the room and used the bedroom extension to call her friend, Jane Willoughby.

Jane was a good friend. Their husbands were best buddies. But Willow knew Jane would rescue her.

When Jane answered, Willow asked quietly, "Jane, this is Willow, can you come and get me? I'm afraid of Frank."

No more conversation was needed. Jane said, "I'm on my way out the door. I'll be there in five minutes."

Willow hung up the phone, gathered up a few clothes, a nightgown, a robe, her toothbrush and a few essentials into a bag. She slipped the bag into her closet and closed the door. She went back out to the living room and sat on the couch. Frank was still in the kitchen cooking and hadn't heard her on the phone. *Thank God for the bedroom extension.*

As he sat eating at the kitchen table, there was the sound of footsteps coming up to their second floor apartment. Willow was relieved to open the door for Jane and her twelve-year-old daughter, Nancy. Turning her back to the kitchen, she pleaded, "Don't leave me here with him. Take me with you."

Jane saw the look of fright in Willow's huge blue eyes, and said, "Of course."

Willow stepped into the bedroom; grabbed the bag from her closet and the three of them turned to leave the apartment. Jane said to Frank, "Willow will be staying with us for awhile." Before there could be any response, they closed the door and headed down the stairs.

In Jane's car, Willow explained how he seemed to go berserk at the word bawling, that he took as balling. "He is just crazy. I don't know what's wrong with him."

Arriving at Jane's house, they discussed sleeping arrangements. Willow would sleep in Nancy's room. Nancy would sleep with her mother and Bill would sleep on the couch.

"Oh no, I can't put him out like that. Please let me sleep on the couch"

Jane's husband Bill walked into the kitchen. "No, I love Franco like a brother," he said, "but, I want to know that he has to go through me to get to you." Bill then went to the garage to look for an old baseball bat. Finding one, he slid it under the couch, his temporary bed.

Bill knew Frank would stop at the bar after work and he wanted to be there when he arrived. "A good man to man conversation is what we need," Bill said, as he stood to greet his friend.

They discussed Frank's quick temper. Bill told Frank that he had to learn to control his own temper years ago or he would have lost Jane.

"I lost one of my biggest accounts at work that day. I was upset. Without the Hamlin account, my paycheck will take a big hit. Even though Willow makes good money, I need to bring in more. If I can't replace the Hamlin account in the next few weeks, I may need to find a new job. Maybe even a new career."

I realize, though, that is no excuse. I know I had no right to take it out on Willow. I'll call her and take her to dinner and hopefully she'll come back home. I really miss her."

"Oh, I'm sorry to hear about losing your big account. Why are you losing the Hamlin's business?" Bill asked

"They have new owners. It sounds like the new owners have a relationship with their own suppliers so they just don't need us anymore."

Oh, that's rough! But, hey man, what were you thinking? You can't be hitting Willow."

"I know." Frank said. "Clearly I wasn't thinking. I was so upset and frustrated. I'll let her know how sorry I am. Really, Bill, you know she means everything to me."

"Good! And the next time you want to take out your frustrations, come over to my house and hit me. At least I can defend myself against you."

"You're so right. Thanks friend. I'll make it up to her. You'll see."

"I hope you can convince her, because I'm sleeping on the couch until she forgives you." Bill joked.

"If it does turn out that you need another job entirely, I can get you on as a carpenter on one of my crews. Have you ever been a carpenter? Do you have any tools, man?"

"Honestly, no, I have never been a carpenter, but I can swing a hammer. No, I don't have tools either. But don't worry, I'm hoping I can replace the Hamlin account with two or three other smaller accounts."

"Willow, there is a phone call for you on line one," said Tina. "It sounds like that handsome husband of yours." Willow had not mentioned anything about the trouble with Frank to anyone at work.

He was handsome with his olive skin, dark brown eyes and nearly black hair, neatly cut to accent his virile chiseled chin. All six feet of him screamed 'heart stealer'. He was a first generation American with both parents coming directly from Italy.

"This is Willow," she said as she answered her telephone extension.

"Honey, I have missed you so much. I love you. Will you do me a favor and have dinner with me tonight? We need to talk. How about if I pick you up at Bill's and take you to dinner tonight? We'll go to Mariachis."

"Hmmm, okay, that sounds nice. Dinner is fine, but I'll meet you there. Is 7:00 o'clock okay?"

"7:00 is good. I'll be there with bells on, and Willow, I can't wait to see you. I'm worthless without you."

After work, Willow changed into a black pencil skirt, and a light blue satin blouse with long sleeves. She cinched a black belt around her tiny waist. That was the last of the clean clothes she had at Bill and Jane's.

They both pulled into the parking lot at the same time so he opened the door for her and they entered the restaurant together.

Frank wore a long sleeved black sweater, under a tan suede blazer. He was wearing new jeans and cowboy boots.

It was a restaurant they had frequented before so ordering was easy. They started with margaritas and a bowl of tortilla chips and salsa.

Dinner was even more delicious than usual. She loved the food there. They declined chocolate cake for dessert. But he knew how much she enjoyed her favorite ice cream drink. He ordered her a Brandy Alexander and ordered a Grasshopper for himself.

As he took the tiny spoon served with the drink to begin his, Frank continued with his crusade to recapture her heart.

"I will forever be sorry for scaring you. It will never happen again I promise."

Willow could tell by the big tears that began to stream down his cheeks how sorry he was. He hadn't had a chance to tell her about losing his biggest account at work. But Bill had mentioned it to her back at the house.

"With the loss of the Hamlin account, if I don't find another account to replace them, I'll have to find a new job. It won't be easy but I have a couple of good leads on big accounts so don't worry. I'm sure we'll be fine. If worse comes to worse, Bill offered me a job as a carpenter on one of his crews."

Willow believed him when he promised it would never happen again. She still had a hard time believing it had happened in the first place. She knew he loved her. *How could someone who loved her hurt her?*

Frank had always done well in sales because, as his friends at work teased, "He could charm the scales off a fish."

So it was no surprise that even before their waitress brought their bill, Willow had agreed to go back home to their apartment. Since she had her own car they both drove home to their apartment. Most of her clothes were still at the apartment and she always did keep an extra toothbrush. She could pick up her other things from Bill and Jane's over the weekend.

As she entered their apartment just behind Frank, she was surprised to see that he had clearly just vacuumed and everything looked to be nice and clean.

They had another cocktail at home and very soon were rolling in the bed having great make-up sex. Willow had never felt so loved.

At the age of twenty-two, Willow was in love with her job, in love with the warm weather in Southern California and madly in love with Francesco. She felt terrible that he lost his biggest account. She also knew it had been crippling for his sizeable ego.

Living in California the past few years had been a welcome respite for her. She had grown up in South Dakota where the harsh winters were brutal.

Aside from the often-severe winters, Willow had a charmed childhood. In a rural setting just outside the city limits of Watertown, Willow's parents and grandparents lived in two separate houses on a shared twenty acres. A bridge stood over the stream that ran between the houses making it easy to walk or run from one house to the other.

The houses didn't face each other. The front doors of both

houses faced east. They were able to watch the sun come up in the morning. From the back porch of either house, they could marvel at the wondrous South Dakota sunsets.

Both houses had their own driveways and their own lawns and gardens, with plenty of tall trees between the houses. But the houses were close enough so on the rare occasion that Willow's mother wasn't home, the girls could go to Grandma Nellie's house when they came from school.

Willow was the one who most often went to Grandma's after school for cookies and milk-coffee even when her mom was home. She loved her Grandma and Grandpa. They would typically drop everything when she walked in the door. Grandma would declare it was time for a coffee break.

Willow's grandparents had built both houses when they purchased the land many years before Willow's parents were even married. Both grandparents loved trees and conveyed that love to their daughter Mildred. So when Mildred started dating a man whose hobby was the study and conservation of trees, Mildred and her parents knew Duncan was the one for her.

Her grandparents had hoped their only child, would marry a man from the area who would see the benefits of living on their acreage and that they would raise a family in the larger of the two houses.

Not only did Duncan want his new wife and their future children to move into the larger house on the property, he wanted to plant a tree as each child was born.

He planted one tree per year for each daughter. Its not surprising that each of the girls was named for a different tree.

Willow, Linden and Marigold were all welcomed by the planting of a new young tree.

Willow couldn't imagine having to tell her family that Frank had hit her. Who does that? No one she knew, that was for sure. On the phone she had assured them that they would all love Frank once they met him. She sensed they were skeptical. If they knew about his temper, they would never welcome him into the family.

A couple of weeks passed and Willow noticed that her breasts were feeling fuller and much more tender than normal. Two of the ladies at work had shared that was how they first knew they were pregnant.

Am I pregnant? The idea frightened, but also excited her. She made an appointment with her doctor.

"Well, Mrs. Rossi, I have good news, I hope." Said Dr. Young. "You are pregnant. Your baby is due the end of April." After being given prescriptions to keep her and the baby healthy, she left the doctor's office and drove home to think.

This changes everything. Willow's mind was spinning. A baby! How exciting! A child I can love and who will love me back. With a baby, Frank's temper will surely mellow. She truly didn't want to raise a baby with no father so leaving him was way at the end of the list of options for her.

Willow called Frank at work, "Can you meet me for lunch at Dillon's Diner? I have something to talk to you about."

"Sure! This is a perfect day to meet you for lunch. I'll see you in a half hour." She felt like his reaction to her news would be a gauge as to how the rest of their marriage would be.

"Oh, honey, that is wonderful news. You'll be a great mommy.

You know that I don't get to see my other daughters very often and I really miss seeing them. It's the best news I've heard in a long time."

They had entertained his daughters a couple of times but it had been awkward for everyone. All three girls, the oldest being eight, were uncomfortable spending time with their dad and his new wife. Their grandmother, Francesco's mother, believed that a man had only one wife, his first wife. Therefore, in her mind, Willow did not exist. The hostility the girls showed to Willow might have come from her.

Willow hoped, maybe now, with a new baby coming, it would be easier for them all to bond. She hoped his girls would want to see their new baby brother or sister. see more of their father even if he never suggested it.

She hadn't told anyone at work about her pregnancy, but was still working her way around it. The idea of not having this baby was never considered. But she would tell them in her own time.

Chapter 3

Francesco and Bill spent the morning picking out new tools and a carpenter's belt. Since Frank was reluctant to spend a lot of money having recently left his job, Bill paid for most of the tools.

"You can't walk on to any worksite with a brand new tool belt and tools," Bill stated. "We have to make them looked used."

"So how do we do that?" asked Frank.

"We'll use a little bleach, a little grease, and maybe some acid and then rub it all in and rub it all off. Maybe we could spill a little soda pop on the belt."

Like two little boys making mud pies, these two grown men worked and played most of Saturday afternoon. Soon, with Sunday and Monday to dry out the tool belt, and time for the bleach and acid to age, Frank was ready for a real test on one of Bill's construction crews. Monday he would join the carpenter's union.

Frank's first day at his new job went well. He was naturally a great schmoozer, but he had been humbled. A humble schmoozer made him even more likeable. The crew took to him right away. They understood it had been some time since Frank had worked on a crew, and they were more than willing to give him pointers. They all liked him.

Francesco took to carpentry like he had taken to sales. The other apprentices liked him as well as those who were Journeymen carpenters. He really enjoyed the different work sites. At first the work was mostly outside. Soon, watching a building come to life from nothing, and knowing that he had a part in it was a new experience. He liked it and he really liked the guys on the crew.

Willow's waist was thickening. She was choosing her clothing carefully as she dressed for work each day. She still wasn't ready to share her pregnancy with her co-workers.

As Willow's baby began to grow within her, the need to protect this child and bring it into a safe world was foremost in her mind. She hoped and prayed Frank's temper was not going to be a problem any more. He promised it wouldn't. How she hoped she could believe him.

Frank wasn't stopping at the bar very often. He was hungry now after a day of physical work and came home for supper. Willow always made a good meal.

She loved cooking for a hungry man. One night after dinner she said she'd serve dessert in the living room. "I have something serious I want to talk to you about."

Frank sat with his eyes wide and his mouth open as he

wondered what was coming. Willow was smiling so he didn't worry that it was anything bad.

Once they were both seated on the couch in the living room, Willow began. "Now that you have some experience as a carpenter, maybe you could be a carpenter in South Dakota. My cousin owns a construction company. I'm sure he'd hire you.

"I could get a job in Watertown. If they wouldn't hire me until after our baby is born, we could still make it because the cost of living is so much less in South Dakota than it is here in California. And as far as the baby is concerned, we'd have lots of free babysitters with both my sisters and my parents in Watertown."

Willow could hardly breathe waiting for his response. She thought she might faint as she watched him considering her suggestion. Frank looked very serious but calm. He raised his eyebrows and cleared his throat. "Well, my dear Willow, maybe that is a good idea. Let's sleep on it."

The next day after work, he came right home and seemed excited. During supper he said, "I know it would make you feel better to have your sisters around the baby. You can check out apartment rentals and see if your cousin really might have a job for me."

She didn't know it, but Frank had just been informed that the crews were breaking up and he would be working with a different crew the next week. It was a crew he did not feel good about.

Willow exhaled and smiled broadly. Her heart was dancing. She would have her sister, Lindy, check out rentals. She was ready to give her two-week notice at work and hoped Frank would give his two weeks as well. This meant she could raise her baby around family in South Dakota. In her opinion, her old home state was a much better place to raise a baby.

~

Olivia, one of Willow's co-workers insisted on giving Willow a baby shower before she left. Willow was honored and had been quite relieved that at work, finally they all knew about the baby.

Olivia invited all the women and a few of the men at work over to her house for the baby shower. It would be Friday, Willow's last day on the job.

The afternoon of the shower both of Olivia's children came home from day care with chicken pox. No one wanted to expose Willow to the chicken pox. Olivia's husband was a nurse and could stay with the kids. The party just couldn't be at Olivia's house.

So at the last minute their plans were changed. The shower was now at Vinnie's bar and Grill after work, just a few blocks away. Vinnie's had a room in the back where the group could be alone.

Olivia had called Vinnie's and explained that it was a last minute change of plans and asked if their party room was available. It was. Big relief!

She ordered several trays of appetizers to be served as they arrived. She was sure that everyone, except for Willow would have a drink or two.

The gifts for the baby were wonderful. Sleepers, soft blankets, rattles, crib bumpers, and crib sheets. All were in yellow or green so they would work for either a girl or a boy. Willow hadn't realized what loyal friends she was leaving. She hadn't realized how much they all loved her and wished the very best for her.

After the party her co-workers helped her carry the gifts to the car. She hoped Frank would be home to carry the gifts upstairs to their apartment.

When she got home Frank was in the bathroom so she dropped the first load of gifts on the couch and rather than wait for him, she went downstairs to get more. She was able to get it all in three trips but she was exhausted.

As Willow was catching her breath, Frank came out of the bathroom, picked her up off the couch and threw her against the wall. He picked her up and slapped her face, first on one side and then the other and tossed her back onto the couch.

"You haven't been at Olivia's. My buddy from the bar said he sitting at Vinnie's earlier when you walked in. Why did you lie to me?"

Willow's first thought was making sure nothing was broken. She didn't think anything had happened to put the baby in danger. She thanked God that she wasn't in pain and her baby was still safe.

She didn't scream or cry. She calmly looked Frank straight in the eye and explained Olivia's children came home with chicken pox so at the last minute they moved the party to Vinnie's. If his bar buddy had stayed long enough to notice, he would have seen her co-workers all in the back room having their baby shower.

"What is wrong with you Franco? Why do you always go for my face?"

Crying now, Frank admitted, "You are so beautiful, Willow. I guess I am afraid that I can't keep you. If you are not mine, I feel like I want to make sure no one else wants you."

Willow realized this was not the conversation of a sane man, but she didn't want to risk angering him anymore. By now he was looking through the gifts and he just kept crying.

"I'm so sorry, Willow. I love you so much. I wouldn't blame you if you left me. But if you leave me I'll never survive. I'll just kill myself. Please don't leave me. Please forgive me. You better get a package of frozen peas out and hold it on your face"

Willow was tired and needed to get some sleep. She was touched, though, by all the tears, and how sorry Frank was for his bad behavior. She didn't want him to kill himself.

Saturday morning, when Willow woke up, she noticed her shoulder hurt a little from where he had shoved her against the wall. But as she walked into the bathroom and saw herself in the mirror, she cried. Her entire face was purple. She could hardly find her eyes for all the purple.

Her plans for Saturday morning had been to do laundry and get boxes for packing. Their apartment-complex had a community laundry facility. Chances of meeting others in the laundry room were great. She knew if anyone saw her they would be horrified. She had never seen anyone's face look so purple.

Willow knew it was finally past time to talk. "I made breakfast if you're hungry."

Frank looked relieved and sat down to eat. Willow had already eaten. While he ate, she began, "Frank, one thing that has to happen is that you need to find some counseling. If we're going to

South Dakota and live around my family, and have a child, you are going to have to get control of your temper and your jealousy. You're going to really hurt me some day and may even hurt the baby. Is that what you want?"

"Oh, baby, I don't want to hurt you. I don't want to hurt our baby. And I really do want to start a new life in South Dakota. I'll do whatever you want. If that's counseling, I'll do it.

Willow smiled. She understood his heart. She knew he didn't want to hurt her, but he needed help. There was no point in calling a counselor for an appointment for him now when they were leaving in less than a week. Hopefully they would find a good counselor in Watertown.

She sorted the laundry and set the baskets on the coffee table and told Frank he would have to do the laundry. It was obvious to him as well, so he gathered the quarters from their quarter jar, the detergent, the baskets of dirty clothes, and headed for the laundry room.

Frank would have to go get boxes to pack for the move. She would not be able to leave their apartment for several days.

Chapter

4

Except for their avocado cut velour couch and their large console television, the apartment they had lived in was partially furnished, so they didn't need a big U-Haul truck. An enclosed trailer they could tow behind their '65 black Thunderbird was plenty big enough. Their clothing, kitchenware, various knick-knacks, and other personal items wouldn't take long to pack. Neither of them had winter coats or boots so those things would have to be purchased in South Dakota.

Willow knew from the past that it would take at least four days for her face to heal. Her shoulder was already better. She also knew it would take about three days of driving to get there and they weren't yet ready to leave. Her face would be healed before they arrived in South Dakota.

She knew he would never let her drive on their trip across country, nor she did she want to drive towing a trailer. She had driven very little lately anyway. Just to work and back. Every other place they went together he always drove.

She hoped that he was still in agreement to counseling when they arrived in Watertown. She would not ask her family to refer one but she could find one in the yellow pages once they were there. Until now her family might have had their suspicions but they had never been confirmed by Willow. She wanted so much for them to like him.

At his insistence, she had married him without waiting for any of her family to meet him. She wanted some confirmation from them that she hadn't been foolish by giving in to him when he was in a big rush to get married. She wanted them to see that he did love her. She wanted them to love him. They never would even give him a chance if they knew how violent he had been and how often he had hurt and bruised her.

All her family had wished for Willow and her new husband and unborn baby to be closer, so when they had received word that they were moving home and would arrive in about a week, they were thrilled.

Her unknown husband, Francesco Rossi, would soon be there. From what Willow had shared, they knew he was a full-blooded Italian. They knew that he'd been in a very big hurry for them to get married for no apparent reason other than he wanted them to be married. Lindy, her sister, hoped it wasn't because he wanted to 'own' her.

Her sisters, Linden and Marigold and their husbands were all hoping they would learn to like him if not learn to love him. So far they had their doubts, but Willow's mother Mildred, asked the family to give him the benefit of the doubt. After all, he was the father of Mildred's unborn grandchild. Willow was a bright young woman and if she loved him, he must be a great guy. "Lets all keep an open mind." Mildred said.

~

During the last miles of the trip, Willow's excitement was building. Frank had been in a good mood the whole trip. Willow continued to be amazed that 'morning sickness' had not been a problem for her at all. She thanked God every day for the absence of morning sickness.

Earlier in her life she had been in the habit of praying and talking to God, but since she had moved to California, not once had she even been to church. She had no idea where the nearest Lutheran Church was. Frank drove everywhere, so she didn't really feel confident in driving herself to unfamiliar destinations.

Living in California with Frank, they had rarely discussed attending church. He had been raised Roman Catholic. She had been raised Lutheran. Neither was willing to go to the other's church and neither wanted to go alone, so they didn't go.

But Willow knew that at home in Watertown she would be expected to attend the Lutheran Church with her family and would happily submit to their wishes. She had wanted to get reacquainted with God for a long time. Soon that would happen.

Maybe she'd find answers once she had that renewed relationship. She should have asked God what He thought about marrying Francesco and asked Him to bless their marriage.

If she hadn't been so rushed, she might have. It was a little late now. She suspected what God's answer would have been if she had asked Him. She hoped maybe He could still make some good come out of it. Even with all Frank's faults, she did love him.

Chapter 5

With a U-Haul trailer in tow, their black Thunderbird pulled into Linden and Lyle's farm driveway mid morning. "You made pretty good time," Lyle said. He had seen them drive in and was there to meet their car. "After you called yesterday, we didn't expect you until mid afternoon."

Linden had just lifted both boys out of the bathtub after their Saturday bath. It was an earlier bath than normal because of the anticipated arrival of Willow and Franco.

She heard their dog welcoming visitors and knew it had to be them. Wanting to hurry out to welcome Willow and Frank she left the boys to get themselves dressed before they come out to see Aunt Willow and their new uncle.

Willow fought tears when she hugged Linden. They hadn't seen each other in years. They had always been close until Willow moved away to California. She felt safe now. She knew that her baby would be safe. There were many reasons for her happy tears.

As had been discussed, for the next few days, while Willow

and Frank looked for an apartment to rent, they were welcome to stay in the basement bedroom at Lindy and Lyle's.

Willow hoped the family would accept Frank. This was Saturday morning, so they had the weekend for the family to get acquainted and for both of them to recover from the trip. Their luggage was carried in and taken to the basement bedroom.

"Come in and let me get you something to eat. You must be hungry after your long trip".

Willow answered, "What I really need before anything else is the bathroom. I'll bet Frank does too.

Linden had saved the newspapers from the last few days, so as soon as they relaxed a bit and caught up, they could check for available apartment rentals.

Willow would call her cousin, Todd, to see if he had room on one of his construction crews for Frank to work as an apprentice. She had written to Todd about the possibility but knew Todd would need to meet Frank. He'd also have to acquaint him with the different laws and building codes in South Dakota.

"How are you feeling Willow? Have you felt the baby move yet? We'll need to set up an appointment with a doctor as soon as you get settled." It seemed like rapid-fire questions from Linden, but Willow knew it was all based in love.

Willow smiled, "I'm feeling just great. I have gained a few pounds, gotten a little thick around the middle, but I am surprised and pleased that I haven't had any morning sickness. Lindy, were you bothered with nausea in the first months?"

"I was lucky, and if you haven't experienced it either, it must be our good genes. No, I didn't have it with either of the boys.

Mom is coming out this afternoon. We can see what her history was on her pregnancies."

"How is mom? I'm so glad to be here and be able to share our baby with her and dad. I thought maybe they would be here this morning."

"She had a hair appointment. She wanted to look her best for your arrival." Even though Willow and her mom had never been close, Mildred always felt appearances were worth everything.

"Oh great! We've been traveling for days, and looking pretty scruffy, but knowing her, she wants to be perfect. Glad she's doing well. How about Dad? Will he come with her this afternoon?"

"Yes, but it'll be later this afternoon when they arrive" Lindy announced. "Mari and Jason will be coming out for supper, a potluck of sorts. They'll all bring something. We've missed you so much, Willow. And of course, they want to meet Francesco."

Lindy turned to wink at Frank, who was smiling and trying to absorb it all. Suddenly everyone seemed to be looking at him. It was his turn to say something.

"I've been anxious to meet everyone. It is good to meet your family, Linden. I knew you would all be wonderful people. Willow is a reflection of her great family.

Willow smiled proudly. Surely they would see why she loved him. Since they arrived, Willow had been thanking God. She thanked him for getting them to South Dakota to her family safely.

She felt relief. She knew that here she would be attending Calvary Lutheran church where the entire family had membership. The church was where her parents had been married and all the girls baptized. It was where they had all attended Sunday school. Willow's two sisters had both been married in that church. Her new baby would be baptized, just as she had been about two weeks after birth.

In California, Frank had not wanted to attend church. He had been raised a Roman Catholic. In fact, to fulfill his mother's dream, he even tried seminary. But he gave it up when both he and the seminary leaders realized his heart was not in it.

If Frank wished to attend a Catholic church now, she was open to attending with him occasionally. She honestly didn't know if he would come with her and the rest of the family to Calvary Lutheran. She hoped he would but she wouldn't push him.

"Willow!" Marigold was running towards her while Jason finished parking their Suburban. They hugged each other tightly. Willow was closer to her sister Linden, but she loved Mari very much.

Just after they arrived, Willow's mom and dad pulled into the driveway. Willow waited for them to park standing ready with hugs. Duncan had been saving a big strong hug for his middle daughter who had been gone much too long.

They were an attractive family. All three sisters were blonde, with blue eyes, slim and attractive, but in Frank's opinion, neither sister came close to Willow's beauty.

Mildred and Duncan had lived just outside of Watertown, all their married life. They had been surprised when their middle daughter, just before she turned twenty, announced her intention to move to California to find a job.

Linden was the first sister to marry and Lyle already owned

his land, so Marigold, the youngest sister and her husband Jason were the logical ones to move into their grandparent's larger home. Their parents had moved into the smaller house after grandma and grandpa passed away.

Sadly they both passed away before Mari and Jason were married. Grandma Nellie died first with heart failure. Less than a year later, Grandpa followed her to heaven. They all felt that he just didn't have the will to live without his beloved Nellie.

Before her original trip to California, Willow had contacted cousins in California who would allow her to stay with them until she found a job and an apartment. She wanted to see more of the country than she had seen in South Dakota. In 1968 getting away from home had been an overwhelming urge.

Through the newspaper, she located a young man who wanted to go west, but wanted a rider to help drive in order to travel straight through.

Willow had never met the young man she would ride with, until she climbed into the car with him to leave for California. She trusted people to be good and decent. She had spoken with him on the phone and that was enough for her. Luckily, he was a nice young man and they continued to be friends long after their trip together.

Sadly, moving away meant that she would miss all the holidays and special days with the family unless she found a really good job and could afford several flights back and forth. It had broken all their hearts.

Willow was back home now with a new husband and they were thrilled to see her, but withholding judgement about him. He would have to prove himself.

"So nice to finally meet you Frank." Mildred half-hugged him and gave him a sincere enough smile. "Welcome to South Dakota!"

"Thank you. It's nice to be here. I'm so glad to finally meet both of you." Frank answered as he shook Duncan's extended hand with a strong grip.

Supper went well. They served it buffet style. Lindy set out all the wonderful casseroles and fried chicken. There was plenty of food. Lyle announced there was beer or wine for whoever wanted. He didn't push it because Mildred was against alcohol. No one wanted to be on her 'naughty' list. The daughters didn't drink anything but water with their meal. The sons-in law each had a beer. Everyone knew that when Mildred and Duncan left, the girls would get into the wine.

Frank was charming as only he could be. The men all liked him and didn't understand why the sisters were suspicious of him. It had been a hurry-up wedding in Vegas a year ago now. The sisters didn't trust anyone who would do that to their Willow. What could have been the hurry? Clearly she wasn't pregnant at that time so it wasn't that.

After supper, when they were cleaning up the table the real conversation started. Duncan and Mildred had left right after the meal as they wanted to get home before dark.

"My baby doctor was wonderful, Willow. I can call him Monday, if you want, or give you his phone number," offered

Lindy. "Or Marigold's doctor was a woman. You liked her didn't you Mari?"

"Yes, she was terrific! A woman baby doctor had been kind of a new thing for Watertown, but she made me feel like I was the most important person in her life. When it's your first baby, that's a very comforting feeling. You might consider using her." Mari said, as she turned to get her pregnancy doctor's phone number out of her purse.

"I have only seen my doctor in Whittier twice. I did call him and ask for a referral in Watertown. I wrote it down, but I don't think he knew much about this doctor," Willow answered. "I guess it depends on where we find to live and how far away the doctor is. At least until I am more at ease in finding my way around town, and if we'll be able to get a second car."

"I put a few days of real estate want ads from the local paper on the table in the laundry room. They always include a section of rentals, if that's what you and Frank want," Lindy motioned to the laundry room.

"There is so much for us to discover and to arrange. I'd like to find a place to rent, as soon as possible. If its not furnished, we'll need to hit some garage sales and second hand stores for furniture.

"Have either of you seen Todd?" Willow asked. "When I called him and asked if he could use Frank on one of his crews, he said he'd like to meet him first, but he was sure he could put him on at least part-time. We'll call him tomorrow and let him know we're here."

Frank came to the dining room where the sisters were sitting. "We need to find a space where we can put things so we can unload the trailer. We need to return it to U-Haul tomorrow if they're open on Sundays.

"Lyle, will you come out here please." Lindy called to Lyle as he came from the room where the men had been visiting. "There might be room in the extra room off the back entryway to put their couch and the TV. If there isn't enough room for their boxes, do you have space in the shed for the boxes, just temporarily?"

"There is always a chance of mice out there even if the boxes are taped good. If we can find room somewhere in the house, their things will be safer. Frank, let's go out and look at what's in the trailer and then decide." Jason, want to come with?"

"Sure," Jason answered, "be right with you. Where are we going?"

Lyle and Frank were already out the door. Mari answered that they were going to unload the trailer. Jason grabbed his jacket and was out the door.

In a few minutes, Willow looked out the large picture window to see the couch being hauled into Lindy's back room. After shuffling the furniture already in there back against the wall, they agreed they would be able to get boxes and all into that room where it would be safe from the elements and safe from rodents.

Lindy normally used it for a craft room but she had no plans to use it in the near future. Their things would be fine there and would not be in anyone's way.

Chapter

6

Lindy was a full time mom and farm wife. She would help them find a place to live. Willow hoped to have a couple of rental places lined up so they could go look as soon as Frank returned from returning the U-Haul.

Before Frank left to return the trailer on Monday morning, Willow called Todd, to see if he'd be around to meet Frank later that day.

Todd, being a second cousin, who admired Willow a lot, said, "Sure! Bring him by my office around noon. I'll plan to meet him there. We can talk a little and we'll see which project he would feel most comfortable joining. I look forward to meeting him. Tell him to be ready to start tomorrow after he visits the Carpenter's Union. Welcome home, Willow!"

"Thanks Todd! You're the best!" Willow said as she hung up.

Turning to Frank, she smiled and relayed the conversation. "So, depending on what time you get back here from U-Haul, it might be time to go to Todd's office. We'll wait and do apartment shopping this afternoon. I'll see what I can line up for us to look at while you're gone."

"Okay, Lindy, we need you to give Frank directions to get to U-Haul and then later to Todd's office."

Watertown wasn't a huge city in the 1970's so directions to anywhere in town weren't that difficult. Frank was quick to understand and was on his way to return the U-Haul trailer.

Willow looked over the real estate ads, focusing immediately on the rentals. There were not many that looked affordable. But it would sure help if Frank could already begin working tomorrow.

There was one. It was a large one bedroom, one bathroom house, with a detached garage. The reason the rent was low, was because it was about one hundred yards from the railroad tracks. There were very few houses in the neighborhood.

Willow called and made an appointment for them to see it that afternoon. The tracks were not used much but they were still in working condition and were used occasionally.

She was happy that it would be after Frank met with Todd. Maybe he'd have a better idea about his wages and hours so they would know how much rent they could handle.

Frank fit in with Todd's crew, as Willow knew he would. People always liked him. There were many things construction wise, that were done differently in South Dakota than they had been in California, but Frank was a willing and fast learner.

~

During her pregnancy, Willow had read about all the things that could go wrong and common birth defects. *Who am I that I should be fortunate enough to have a healthy baby?* "Please God, if it be your will, bless my precious baby with good health."

Frank and Willow rented the one bedroom house near the railroad tracks. The bedroom was large enough for the crib to be set up against the far wall. With the help of Willow's sisters and mother, most of the necessary baby supplies and equipment were purchased. She was also thankful for the gifts from her baby shower in California. For now it was all stacked in the crib until she bought a chest of drawers for the baby.

Todd kept a close eye on Frank's work and found that the other men liked working with him and gave him good reviews. In fact, in a few weeks, Smitty, one of the men on his crew, who lived very close, offered to pick Frank up for work and bring him home so Willow could have the car most days. Now she would be able to go grocery shopping, get to doctors appointments and begin to get things ready for the baby.

That meant also, that if the whole crew stopped for a beer or two, Smitty and Frank stopped. If the crew didn't stop, which was most of the time, Frank was delivered home right after work. It was a much different situation for Frank, and it worked well for their new lives.

Willow loved being close to her family and went to church with them most Sundays. Frank was always too tired or wanted to be home to watch some game on TV, but never joined the family at Calvary Lutheran. It didn't set well with her family members but they agreed not to make a big deal of it.

As the weeks passed, Willow spent a lot of time with her family, but made a real effort to be home when Frank was home.

His temper seemed to be mostly under control and Willow felt safe for the first time in many months.

Her baby was due towards the end of April, so her appointments had been weekly during April.

"Well, Willow, everything is more than ready. If you don't have your baby during the night, come to the hospital at 7:00 in the morning and we'll break your water and help things along a little." Dr. Anderson said with a smile.

Willow went immediately to visit Linden. "I'm going to have a little May basket tomorrow."

Linden hugged her. " That's exciting, but how do you know?" questioned Linden

"Dr. Anderson is going to induce labor. I have to be there at 7:00 AM so he can do it after he does hospital rounds. It's Saturday so Frank won't have to worry about missing a day of work.

As soon as Willow got home she called the site where Frank was working and left a message for him to call home.

The phone rang in just a few minutes. "Hi honey, what did the doctor say? Is everything okay?" asked Frank.

"Yes, everything is fine. But Dr. Anderson is going to induce labor tomorrow morning. I have to be there at 7:00 A.M. I just wanted you to know in case Todd wanted you to work tomorrow; you can explain why you can't. Isn't it exciting? The day has finally arrived."

"Well, if he induces you at seven, what time does he expect the baby to arrive?" Frank asked.

"It's hard to know," Willow answered. "He said he would guess the earliest would be about noon. Why?"

"Well, Smitty has been telling me about tomorrow being the state fishing opener. I just bought my license. We could go fishing at 6:00 A.M. and I could still easily be at the hospital before noon. Do you think Linden could take you to the hospital?"

Willow couldn't answer right away. Her heart sank. "I don't know. I'll call her." Her voice was fading.

"Don't worry, honey. I'll be there before the baby arrives."

Without responding, Willow hung up the phone. She had to wait a few minutes to regain her composure before she called Linden.

"Yes, of course, I can take you. Lindy responded. "The South Dakota fishing opener, huh? No problem. I'll be there about 6:30."

Being on time or early was almost a religious characteristic that Mildred had instilled into all three of her girls, and it had stuck.

At 6:30 sharp Lindy and Lyle both came to pick her up for the drive to the hospital. Willow tried to push to the back of her mind, how disappointed she was that they had to do this at all. *How could Frank miss taking her to give birth to their first baby?*

Once Willow was admitted into the maternity ward and comfortable in her hospital room, Lindy reappeared bearing a dozen red roses. They were beautiful. Lindy had always gotten flowers from Lyle each time she had a baby and she wanted Willow to have flowers as well.

"Thank you so much. I love them." Lindy and Lyle left saying they would stay in close contact. Willow was embarrassed. She knew Lindy didn't trust Frank to bring her flowers after fishing. Neither did she.

In the past weeks when Willow had been home with a car available, she had made several trips to the local library. She had been researching information on men who battered women. Her knowledge was very personal. She needed to find out more. She hoped to find out what to expect and how to fix whatever was wrong with Frank.

She had been shocked to read that often men don't batter their wives because they have been drinking, but rather they drink so that they will have an excuse to do the battering.

She also learned that, once a batterer, always a batterer. With the proper motivation, a man can be on his good behavior for a time, but eventually, without serious therapy or a 'come to Jesus' moment, he will batter again. In other words, an abusive event is never going to be a one-time thing.

She was distressed to read that in most cases each battering incident became more violent than the previous one. Which is why so many ended in fatalities.

As Willow lay in her bed at St. Joseph's Hospital, she had time to think about Frank and about their marriage. She had no idea if she was about to give birth to a son or a daughter. As she waited for Frank and for signals from her body and the nurses that a baby was imminent, she had time to silently pray in her room.

After praying, she felt that if her baby was a girl, it was a sign from God that she would be raising her on her own in the future. But if she had a boy, it would be a sign that they would continue to be a family.

At 10:30 that morning, Frank walked though the door of her hospital room. She didn't want to belabor the fact that he missed driving here to the hospital, so she didn't mention it. But she also didn't ask him if he had fun, or if he caught any fish. She didn't care.

"How are you doing?" Frank asked

"Good, I've just started with contractions so I guess it will be awhile before we see our baby. But they did say that things can change quickly once we get started."

"Pretty flowers! Did Lindy bring them?" asked Frank.

"Yes, Lindy and Lyle thought I should have pretty flowers on such a big day." Frank didn't comment.

Just before noon, the pastor from Calvary Lutheran came to visit and say a prayer for an easy birth and a healthy baby. Willow appreciated his visit and drew great comfort in knowing her delivery and her baby were covered in prayer. She had to introduce the pastor to Frank because he had never been to church with her. Willow asked the pastor about getting the baby baptized in a couple of weeks.

Mildred called her room after lunch to say she and Duncan were waiting to hear that the baby was here, and they would come as soon as they could after the baby's arrival.

Marigold was going to do the same, but Lindy stopped in for a few minutes just to see how things were progressing. Willow was pretty sure she wanted to see for herself that Frank had finally arrived.

"Did you catch any fish?" Lindy asked Frank.

"I did not. My buddy, Smitty did catch three. He had a cooler of ice to drop them in so he could wait to clean them when he got home. But it was fun and something I have never experienced before. Now I have my South Dakota residents license so I can go again."

"Good for you!" Lindy replied, trying to hide her disappointment that could easily become contempt for this man.

It was just after 7:00 P.M when Willow gave birth to a beautiful little girl. She had all ten finger and ten toes and a full head of dark hair.

"Congratulations, you have a beautiful baby girl." Dr. Anderson said. The nurses took her away to clean her up and then before long she was wrapped in a blanket and placed on Willow's chest.

Dr. Anderson burst into the waiting room to find Frank. "Congratulations, Mr. Rossi, you have a wonderful, healthy baby girl. You can go and see your wife and baby now." In the early 1970's fathers were not allowed in the delivery room.

Frank hurried into Willow's room to see their new baby girl. "Oh, look at all that dark hair! She's beautiful." Frank exclaimed and gave Willow a kiss on the forehead.

"Do you want to hold her?" Willow asked.

"I can hold her later," Frank said, "I'll go out and get Linden and your parents. Mari might be here by now too. I called Lindy about an hour ago, when the nurse came out and said it wouldn't be much longer. They'll all want to hold her."

For the next hour there were 'oohs and aahs' from everyone. She clearly was the most beautiful baby girl any of them had ever seen.

Willow had decided on the name of Anna Maria. She and Frank had discussed names but Frank said Willow could decide.

After three days in the hospital, mother and baby were released. Frank arrived to pick them up. After taking everything from her room to the car, he drove around to the side door where the nurse had instructed him to park.

As the nurse placed little Anna Maria into Willow's arms for the ride home, Willow wondered silently. *How can* they send *this precious baby home with me? I don't know how to take care of a baby.*

There were no infant car seat laws in the early 1970's. It was perfectly normal for the baby to ride in a mother's arms in the car.

Willow's attempt at nursing hadn't gone well in the hospital but the nurses said maybe once they were home and settled in, it might go better. It wasn't any better. It was worse because Anna Maria wasn't getting much milk and now Willow's breasts were beginning to swell. Anna was still hungry and fussing. Willow was in pain. Her breasts were full and her nipples were cracking. She wanted to cry. She was supposed to try to relax but that was not going to happen.

So finally, a week after her birth, Willow called Dr. Anderson. He said, "You have given it a good try Willow. I think its time to feed her with the formula we discussed."

Frank had purchased the suggested formula. Willow had it

ready in a bottle in the refrigerator. She heated it in a pan on the stove. In just a few minutes her precious little girl was happily getting nourishment and it caused no pain to Willow.

At the end of the feeding, Anna Maria slept peacefully and Willow smiled broadly. She loved the contented look on Anna's face as she laid her in the crib.

Baby Anna slept for three hours for the first time since she arrived a week ago. Willow kept checking her to make sure she was still breathing. From that day forward, the household was more peaceful. Willow could finally get things done using two arms instead of one.

She was proud of her pretty baby girl. When she took her to the grocery store, total strangers would stop her and rave about her beautiful baby with all the dark hair. Anna Maria had a beautiful smile with alert big brown eyes. Everyone who looked at her smiled. Blonde haired blue eyed babies were much more common in South Dakota, especially in Watertown.

Chapter 7

Winter had come and gone and Frank had handled it well. Having only lived in Southern California all his life, Willow and her family wondered if he would survive the low temperatures and all the extra clothing required to live there. It was a new adventure for him and he seemed to be enjoying it. Her family was beginning to be less suspicious of him and was slowly giving him the benefit of the doubt.

As a couple, they spent the most time with Lindy and Lyle. Lyle liked Frank a lot, but Lindy was still holding out for better behavior. She wasn't sure she bought Frank's charm.

Cousin Todd, who owned the construction company where Frank worked, continued to be pleased with his work and the crew seemed to like him a lot. They found him to be fun. He worked hard and held up his share of the work on each project.

Anna Maria was a momma's baby. Her daddy wasn't one to pay her a lot of attention. She was even cuter now as a soon to be toddler. Her dark little curls gently framed her enchanting face.

Frank's friend Smitty approached him at work. "Can you be a little late for supper tonight? I want to talk to you about something. Call Willow and ask her if we can stop off at the bar for a bit after work."

Frank went into the office to use the phone to call Willow and see if it was okay for him and Smitty to stop off at the bar. This was a huge difference from his behavior in California, where he never asked or let her know he would be late in getting home for supper.

"Don't worry about supper for me. Smitty said maybe we we'll just grab a burger at the bar."

"That's fine. What does he want to talk to you about?" Willow asked.

"I have no idea, honey." Frank responded.

"Have a good time. Don't be too late." Willow decided to make grilled cheese sandwiches and tomato soup for Anna and herself.

It was close to 9:00 P.M. before Frank came home.

"Did you eat?" Willow asked.

'Yes, that bar makes great burgers. I'll take you there sometime."

"So, what was his big news? What did he want to talk to you about?" She asked after Frank walked in, grabbed a beer out of the refrigerator and sat down in his recliner.

"It's a big deal. He has a job offer in Kansas City for a lot more money and they need two carpenters. He wants us to move to Kansas City. We would be paid nearly twice what we earn now. It's a great opportunity for us, Willow."

"Hmmm. We'll have to really think about that Frank," Willow said. "If we do that, the extra money would be nice. But we don't know how much more rent we'll have to pay. I won't have my family to help with Anna. We won't know anyone there but Smitty. I'm not excited about moving at all."

"We've been making it okay with you not working, Willow. And it will be the same in Kansas. So we don't need to worry about babysitters. I can go with Smitty down there and start working. I can look for an apartment or a house for us to rent and come back and get you and Anna."

"Oh, Frank, I don't know. It didn't feel right."

"One of the big reasons I think it's a good idea is because of the company we would work for. It's a huge construction company, known all over the country. There are all kinds of opportunities with this company."

"Maybe you should go there and check it out first." Willow interjected.

"Smitty is going down there next Sunday. I can go with him. It's just two states away. It's not half way across the country like it was when we were in California. Smitty thinks it will take just over six hours to drive, so it can easily be done in one day." Frank continued.

"It doesn't sound that good to me, but we can think about it."

Willow answered. Thinking more, she suggested, "Why doesn't Smitty go and see how he likes it before we pack up and move again. I really don't want to take Anna Maria away from her aunts, cousins and grandparents."

"But Willow, its double the money I'm making now."

"You go with Smitty, and check it out." Willow insisted.

~

Early the following Sunday morning Frank and Smitty headed for Kansas City. Smitty was recently divorced with no children so he was looking at this as his new beginning. He and Frank had really become close friends at work and Smitty hoped Frank would be able to talk Willow into moving.

"Oh, Lindy, I hope Frank won't like it there and will decide to stay here in Watertown."

"Me too, Willow. I have been praying about it. I don't want you to leave. It's been so nice to have you here. We're so in love with Anna Maria. We want to have her close so we can watch her grow. Mom and Dad love having you here too. I know none of us wants to see you go."

Tuesday morning Willow had a call from Frank He was excited. "Willow, you won't believe it! This guy already put us to work. We had to go downtown to join the local carpenters union. We did that yesterday.

Smitty already found himself an apartment. After work today, He is going with me to some places in and out of town to see what might be available for us to rent."

"Did you already decide this is what we're going to do? I thought we'd discuss it when you come home."

"This guy is paying us more than twice what we were getting.

How can we turn it down? It's a nice city. It'll be much warmer in the winter." Even though he hadn't complained about the winter in South Dakota, she knew that winter had been quite a shock to him. They could certainly use bigger paychecks.

Willow loved him and wanted to be fair to him but she hated to leave her family again. She had loved living here. "We have to give our notice to our landlord. You still have to find a place for us to live."

"It makes more sense to stay here and work and find us a place to live. Then I'll come and get you and the baby in a few weeks."

So do you want me to just call our landlord and tell him we're moving? We'll have to pay an extra months rent for not giving notice? Does that make any sense? Do you want me to call and cancel our utilities?"

"Well, baby, I have to live somewhere, I can't live in this cheap motel forever. And I want you guys here with me as soon as possible. I miss you."

"Awe! Well, we miss you too. I guess it does make sense to have you find us a place." She let out a sigh. "Do you like this employer?"

"He's great! He really likes Smitty and me. He said, "We come on time, ready to work.

"Okay, I'll start to get things in motion for moving."

"Great! Love you baby."

"Love you too."

Willow turned to Anna Maria in her walker and said, "Well my sweet Anna, it looks like we're moving to Kansas with Daddy."

Willow was close to her sisters, especially Linden. She was

so thankful to have been here for the short time it was. Whether they would ever be back, she didn't know but for now she felt her duty was to her husband. She hoped her family would understand.

Frank didn't give her time to think about the move. If she hadn't been so pressed for time, she might have thought about putting her foot down and refusing to leave while she had her family to back her up. But during one of his tirades, he told her if she ever left him, he'd burn down Lindy's house with all of them in it. She would rather risk herself than any of them. She didn't think she had a choice but to stay with him.

Chapter

8

It was hard to get her bearings in Kansas City. She didn't have the car often so it really wasn't a problem. Smitty and Frank worked for the same employer on the same project, but Smitty's apartment was in the opposite direction of the house they rented, so she was without a car most days day.

It was fine. They went to the grocery store on weekends. On nice days, Willow would take Anna Maria in her stroller to explore the area. She was happy to discover a shopping center within walking distance.

Willow missed her family and she knew from Lindy's calls that they all missed them as well. But Willow was once again up for the new challenge of adjusting to a new community.

Frank had to leave especially early one Monday morning to travel to a different work site. Willow normally got up to pack his lunch but since it was so early Frank said not to worry about his lunch. He was pretty sure there was a food wagon on that worksite so she hadn't set her alarm.

Willow's butt hit the floor before she was awake. At 5:00 A.M. Willow was being pulled out of bed by her legs.

"Where have you put my new jacket with the company logo on it? I need to wear it today and I can't find it. I've looked everywhere. Even you couldn't have lost it already." He was upset.

"I haven't seen it. I didn't know you got a work jacket. Where did you have it last? Did you even bring it in the house?"

With those words, he turned on his heels and went out to the car. Returning to the house he held the jacket still in the package. He didn't say anything. He just put his jacket on, grabbed his coffee mug and hurried out slamming the door.

Willow was thankful that the racket hadn't awakened Anna Maria. Frank's coffee mug took most of the coffee he had made, so Willow started a fresh pot.

She was still rattled from Frank pulling her out of bed by her feet. She couldn't say he'd been happy and loving since they arrived in Kansas, but at least he hadn't been physically striking her face and bruising her. Her backside was sore now but she knew it would heal.

What she needed now was to get back to spending time in her Bible. During the move she'd found it in a box that had never been unpacked in South Dakota. She tried to digest what had just happened. And she needed some wisdom from her Bible. In years past, she had found wisdom and much comfort in the book of Proverbs.

While he hadn't struck her, it was still unacceptable behavior on his part. As she sipped her coffee, she remembered the research she had done at the Watertown library. One thing she had totally forgotten now popped into her mind. She could almost see the paragraph in the book that talked about how an abuser often separated his spouse from the rest of her family and friends.

Willow sat with her mouth open. How had she let this happen? She had been sweet talked into moving away from the safety of her family. Had he been sold on the move because of the job or, did he embrace the move because he wanted to get her far away from her family's interference and away from their protection? Willow trembled at the thought. Why was she so gullible? But how could she not support her husband? Her head was whirling.

When Frank got home that night, he was charming and jovial. He brought Willow a bottle of her favorite wine. He carried his company jacket with the special logo, over his arm and hung it over the kitchen chair. Seemingly he was proud of the jacket. She didn't know if everyone got a jacket or if he won it. She really didn't care and didn't ask him.

There was no apology for pulling Willow out of bed by her feet earlier, but he had a way of being fun to be around, a way of distracting her. She loved being with him when he was happy and loving. She never confronted him about his violent temper fearing how he would react..

Willow wanted to trust Frank now that another baby was on the way but it was difficult due to his frequent outbursts. What was always in the back of her mind was her desire for a stable family for Anna Maria and the new baby. That meant having both a mother and a father for her children.

Chapter

9

Willow had a small party for Anna Maria's second birthday. She invited two neighbors who also had little girls. She felt lucky to have friends that were just hers. In the past years, except when they were by her family, her only friends were wives of Frank's friends.

She was getting to know both Barbara and Brenda. Brenda's house was right next-door to their house and Barbara was next to her, two doors down.

She made home baked Chocolate cup cakes with chocolate frosting and sprinkles. The little girls each had a vanilla ice cream cone along with their cupcake. The mom's all chose a cone over a dish of ice cream when Willow gave them a choice. There were party hats that stayed on their heads for all of two minutes. When they sang Happy Birthday to Anna Maria, she was shy at first, but smiled wide at the idea of them singing just for her.

Frank came home a little late that night and Willow feared he had stopped at the bar. She didn't want any bad memories connected with Anna Maria's birthday. She saw him drive into the garage and hoped he wasn't drunk. He came in proudly carrying a huge soft teddy bear with black eyes and flexible arms and legs. It was adorable.

Anna Maria loved the bear and named him Bo. A few days before the birthday party, they had discussed birthday presents and both agreed that new clothes for her birthday were enough of a present since she was only two. Still Willow was pleased that he changed his mind and bought the large bear.

Willow's fears about him stopping at the bar were forgotten. She was pleased that she had prepared one of Frank's favorites, beef roast with baked potatoes and buttered green beans for supper.

When he was in a happy mood, Willow made extra effort in every way she could, trying to encourage more good humor. Supper felt romantic. After Anna Maria was read a story and tucked into her bed with a kiss good night on her forehead, Willow went to the kitchen and poured two glasses of wine.

She carried the wine glasses out to the living room and set one in front of Frank as she sat next to him. She wished her sisters could see how happy she was tonight. Frank stopping off for the teddy bear had warmed her heart. She snuggled next to him on the couch.

The following morning, Willow drank her morning coffee, enjoying one of the few moments she would have to herself before Anna was awake. She reflected on the tender way Frank had made love to her last night. She smiled and was glad she was here with him.

As with her first pregnancy, in just a few weeks, Willow noticed her breasts were a little tender and wondered if she might be pregnant again. She waited another week and made an appointment with a doctor without mentioning it to Frank.

Her neighbor Brenda's little girl, Allyson, was in preschool. Brenda was proud to have been taken into Willow's confidence and was pleased to drive her to the appointment and entertain Anna Maria in the doctor's reception area while they waited.

Willow heard the words, "Congratulations, Mrs. Rossi. I have the results of your tests. You are indeed going to have a baby. You should expect to deliver just after Christmas. I will want to see you monthly.

Willow treated Brenda to pie and coffee at the coffee shop next door to the clinic before they headed home. They talked mostly about the baby that would arrive just around Christmas time. It was a good bonding day for both of them.

Willow welcomed Brenda's friendship. Their husbands enjoyed a beer together one Saturday afternoon in their yard. After checking with Frank, Willow invited them over Friday night to play cards so they could get to know each other better. They would put the little girls to bed in Anna's room when they got tired, so no one would need a babysitter.

Frank was less than thrilled to learn of another baby and another mouth to feed but things had been going well for him at work and there shouldn't be any problem, financially at least.

Willow was happy to have gone through a few weeks with no anger outbursts. She was constantly trying to figure out how she could stop his fits of anger. She didn't know how to approach the topic of him getting help. They hadn't discussed it since before they left California.

At first she assumed his anger outbursts were her fault. She must have done something, said something, or looked a certain way that set him off. She thought somehow she deserved his poor behavior. She'd never known of such a man.

But now after years of his outbursts, most of them violent, she had mentally re-hashed every word after every event. She knew it wasn't her fault. She put total blame on him finally. She was pregnant with a second child. She was maturing. But she was concerned about their future.

Most nights after work, Frank came home right after work. It seemed that if he stopped for a few beers, he was more often crabby or agitated. She was always fearful when that happened. Maybe he felt guilty for stopping off.

Like a few nights ago, he arrived home late because of stopping at the bar with the guys from work. The meatloaf and baked potato she had been keeping warm were both dry even with the help of Ketchup. As he sat alone at the table, eating the meatloaf he grew increasingly agitated and without warning, he hammered his plate with his knife until the melamine plate split in three pieces.

He picked it up piece by piece and threw it, meatloaf, ketchup and all, with great venom, into the linen closet next to the table. After flinging the plate with food still on it, he picked up a nearly full half-gallon glass bottle of milk and threw that with a vengeance into the closet.

Willow regretted not closing the door on that closet when she finished putting the clean towels away that afternoon.

Frank seemed to calm down after that and went into bathroom and quickly went to bed. Willow fought tears as she looked at the mess in the closet and on the carpet between the table and the closet.

Besides cleaning up the glass from the milk bottle, she would have to wash all the sheets and towels and really clean the shelving to prevent the smell of sour milk. It looked like the carpeting on the floor was spared.

The racket had awakened Anna Maria but Willow was able to get her back to sleep by rubbing her back and singing a lullaby.

After that she carried the first load to the laundry room. She gave thanks that she had a good collection of quarters. There wouldn't be many residents using the machines if she began tonight. She would do a complete cleaning of the closet while she waited for the laundry. But she was furious to think of the extra work his tantrum had made for her.

Willow knew she would forgive him as soon as he came to sit by her with tears from those big brown eyes running down his face. He was always so sorry. His maple syrup colored brown eyes made her want to believe it wouldn't happen again. But she began to realize it always did. A few weeks of a peaceful household was the most she could hope for in between his tirades.

Chapter

10

Christmas came and went. Willow's due date passed. On New Years Eve she had some contractions, but they stopped. She called her doctor to get his opinion. Because it was the holiday, he said if she made it through the night without more contractions, to come in the day after New Years so they could check her.

She did that and as with Anna Marie, things were more than ready so he said to come early the next morning and he would induce labor.

This delivery went much faster. Ten minutes after they wheeled her into the delivery room, her doctor was in the father's waiting room congratulating Frank on the birth of a healthy baby boy. The meds had no time to work, but it hadn't been a difficult delivery for Willow.

She thanked God for her safe delivery and her healthy baby boy but she was depressed. She couldn't pretend she would be taking her baby boy to a happy and safe home.

Now she was the mother of two little ones, who had only her to protect them. That worry was stealing the joy she should be feeling about her healthy baby boy who still didn't have a name.

As every mother knows the first few weeks of a new baby's life becomes a blur. Anna Maria loved her new baby brother, who was named Antonio. They called him little Tony. Willow thought they should both have Italian names to go with their last name of Rossi. She knew that in time they would be shortened to Anna and Tony, but she liked their names.

Anna Maria called her little brother Tonio. She had to sit on the couch beside her mother when she wanted to hold him. But when she did, her love for him shone like a light from her eyes. She talked to him in her own soft words as she gently touched his face.

Willow kept the car on days Antonio needed to go in for his check-ups and early shots. Her neighbor Brenda was happy to keep Anna Maria for the hour or two during doctor's appointments.

These opportunities were a good bonding time for the little girls as well as Willow and Brenda. The two moms each had shared moments of stress and worry about their little girls, as well as their marriages.

Brenda and her husband's relationship had strengthened but they been through several months of difficulty when Brenda suspected he was cheating on her.

She had prayed hard and never really had her suspicions confirmed but as an answer to her prayers, their marriage bond strengthened. He became more loving and more attentive. Best of all his faith had become deeper. In fact it was at his suggestion that they joined a couple's Bible Study at their church and began to do daily devotions together each evening before they went to bed.

Brenda didn't care what had happened in the past. She thanked God every day for the relationship they had with each other and also with God.

Willow could only dream of such a relationship. She longed for it and began to pray for it. She had been taught the stories of the miracles of Jesus in Sunday school and church all throughout her childhood.

She did believe miracles were still possible, but also knew that God sometimes had other plans. She often wished she had remembered to ask God for his blessing before she married Frank. He might have said, 'No'.

It was a typical Friday and Willow expected Frank to be late. She put their baked chicken in the oven. It would be ready in about an hour. She prepared Tony's his supper, which included minimal table food.

Willow was surprised to see Frank walk in the door from work early. He seemed in a good mood and said they had knocked off early.

It was the last day of March and on his way home, Frank noticed the local Dairy Queen had just opened for the season. He came up with the plan to take Anna Maria to the Dairy Queen.

Willow was pleased that he wanted to do that. Just a daddy and daughter trip to Dairy Queen. She hoped Anna was old enough for it to become a treasured memory for her. It might if he made it a regular thing.

Until now, Frank had not been a hands-on father. In fact, his attitude was much like her fathers had been, that babies and small children were women's work. *Was this new interest in spending time with Anna, the beginning of answers to her prayers?*

Anna was nearly three and rarely had accidents. Just before they left, Willow took her to the bathroom to make sure. As soon as they returned from the bathroom, Frank scooped a smiling Anna up in his arms, and they headed out to the car.

Before they reached the car Frank realized he had left his keys on the table. They turned back to the house. As he walked up the four concrete steps into the house, he stumbled and very nearly dropped Anna. He caught himself and neither of them fell, but that was enough for Anna.

She wanted down and ran to hug her mom's leg. Willow had seen them coming back. As she opened the door she saw the near fall. She was not surprised at Anna's reaction. Anna was a perceptive child with excellent instincts.

It was then that Willow discovered Frank had been off work since noon and he was drunk. Her knees almost buckled. She had almost sent her precious Anna in the car with her drunk father.

The outing was off. Before picking up little Tony to feed him supper, she took the dinner out of the oven and fed Anna. With little Tony in her arms, Willow began to feed him his supper. He was a good eater and would eat it all with enthusiasm. Frank settled on to the couch to read the daily paper with his feet up on the coffee table.

Willow sat back in the chair by the table to feed Tony. When he finished with his bottle, she and Frank would eat.

Before that could happen and without warning, Frank

bounded off the couch and moved over to the table by Willow's chair. He squeezed his hands around her neck and cried. "You have turned my children against me!" His hands tightened around her neck.

She had her baby in one arm and his bottle in the other hand. Anna Maria was clutching the cloth of Willow's shirt. She was screaming with eyes as big as quarters. There was terror in her eyes as she watched her daddy try to squeeze the life out of her mommy.

Something, maybe God, told Willow to just remain calm. Actually she didn't have many choices, but she knew if she showed panic, it would only add to Anna's terror.

Please! God! Don't let him kill me! The kids need me!

In a few seconds that seemed like minutes, with no explanation, Frank dropped his hands from around her neck and went into the bathroom. The minute he did, she got up, went to the phone and dialed 911.

"My husband just tried to strangle me and I want you to come and pick him up." She said.

"What is your address, please?"

Willow gave the dispatcher their address and as she did, she remembered that Brenda and her husband, next door, had a police scanner that they had on most of the time. *Would they hear the call? Would they hear the address?*

After Willow gave the dispatcher the information asked for, she was assured a car had been sent to their house.

When Frank came out of the bathroom, he returned to the couch and picked up the paper. Willow told him his supper was on the top of the stove in the roaster. If he wanted any of that, he was on his own.

In a few minutes she heard a knock on the door. She opened the door to two policemen.

"He just tried to strangle me." She pointed at her neck to show them what she meant. .

As she turned around to point to Frank, she was shocked to see him sitting on the couch holding little Tony in his arms. He looked like a candidate for Father of the Year. She was pretty sure that was the first time he had ever held Antonio.

The police noted the marks on her neck. "We can't throw a man out of his own home ma'am, but we can suggest one of you leave for awhile."

Willow was shocked at what the police said. "I can't leave. It's time for the kids to be put to bed." Willow exclaimed.

"I'll leave." Frank said, and began to rise from the couch.

The police left. Their work here was done.

When Frank left, Willow called Brenda. She knew that Anna hadn't eaten much earlier so she tried to get her to eat a little more. But she just stirred the food around with a spoon. With her free hand, Willow reached to the fridge to get an ice cream sandwich for Anna. She just needed to get something in her tummy.

"Hello," Brenda answered.

"I'm sorry to call so late, Brenda. This is Willow. Do you have your scanner on?"

"No we don't at the moment. I turned it off this afternoon and never turned it back on. Why?" asked Brenda

"Well, I just had to call. The police were just here. At their suggestion, Frank left for a while. I assume he'll come back"

"Why, what's going on? Are you all okay?"

"Yes, we're okay." Willow's voice was cracking. He tried to strangle me. I don't know why he stopped when he did. The cops said someone should leave for awhile and he volunteered."

"What was he mad about?" asked Brenda.

Willow relayed the whole episode.

"Oh, my goodness. Are you going to be all right when he comes home?"

"I have to believe we will. We can't go anywhere, at least not tonight. I just put the kids to bed. Will you pray for us?

Brenda said, "You know, yes, absolutely, I'll pray. We both will. Call me in the morning and let me know that you're okay. And Willow, if you need to call during the night its perfectly fine."

Willow knew of Brenda's strong relationship with God and was relieved to know they would be praying for them.

Antonio's crib had been in their bedroom since they brought him home from the hospital, so he wouldn't wake his big sister at night.

Willow was still awake, when around 1:00 AM, she heard Frank's key in the door. She heard him open the refrigerator and close it again. Soon he turned out the lights and came into the bedroom. With only the light from the closet, he stood quietly over Tony's crib and just stared at his baby boy for several minutes. Willow watched him while trying to look like she was asleep.

What is he thinking? Why is he staring at Antonio? What will he do? Please God! Please protect my baby!

At that moment Willow knew that if they lived through the night, it was absolutely necessary for her and the kids to get away. She had risked her own safety before, made excuses for him. The next time he would kill her. Now she had two precious little ones that needed her.

Suddenly, as if she had a word from God, she knew exactly what she would do. She felt at peace and drifted off to sleep

~

Willow was up very early Saturday morning. She showered and dressed before either of the kids or Frank stirred. While she was alone, she quietly called the airport to find out about flights to Sioux Falls. There was one leaving just after one that afternoon.

Then she called her sister, Linden, in Watertown.

"Lindy, this is me, Willow."

"Willow, hi, you're up early. Are you okay?"

"No, we're not. We need to come there. Is there anyway you can meet the kids and me at the Airport in Sioux Falls this afternoon?"

"Yes, I can do that…"

"And. I hate to ask, but can you also wire the money to the airport for the tickets for us?"

"Yes, I can do that…" *How will I do that? Linden wondered.*

"Oh, good that's wonderful. I can't take the time to go into it now, but there is a plane that leaves here at 1:10 P.M. and gets in to Sioux Falls at 2:20." She gave her the name of the airline and said she'd try to call Linden back later.

Then she called Brenda, next door.

"Good morning Brenda, this is Willow."

"Oh Willow. I've been so worried about you. Are you okay?"

"Yes, we are. For now we are. Listen, Brenda, the kids and I are flying to South Dakota this afternoon. Can you possibly drive us to the airport about 11:30?"

"Yes, I can do that. I'm sorry you feel you have to go and I know you wouldn't go if it weren't necessary. Are you sure you want to leave here at 11:30? It'll take about 45 minutes to get to the airport on a Saturday. If your flight leaves at 1:10, lets plan to leave about 11:00Can you be ready by then?"

"Good. Yes, we'll be ready. Thanks so much, Brenda. See you soon"

As Willow turned around she noticed that Frank was up and in the bathroom. Since it was Saturday, he didn't work. She had no idea if he planned to stay home or go somewhere. *I have to tell him we're leaving.*

Putting on her calmest face, she said, "The kids and I are leaving today to go to Lindy's and Lyle's."

"Oh yeah? How do you expect to do that?"

"Lindy is wiring money for the tickets and we're flying out of here today."

"Oh yeah? Good luck with that!"

With that Frank picked up her purse that was on the floor by the infant seat. He rifled through it to find any cash she had in there. She had a few dollars, and he took them. He missed three dollars she had in a secret compartment.

He opened and slammed all the kitchen cabinet doors. He had already been through all her dresser drawers. As he searched, he discovered a small stash on a high shelf in the kitchen. He put that all in his pocket. She had been saving it for such an occasion.

Frank walked into the bedroom to get his shoes and his jacket. He was leaving. As he stood at the apartment door he turned to Willow and said,

"I understand why you are leaving. I do. And I'm sorry. What time is your flight? I'll come back and take you to the airport."

To Willow it sounded like an invitation to her death. She was pretty sure that getting into the car with Frank today would be the last car ride for all of them. In the past he had threatened to drive them all off a cliff. He threatened her often and demeaned and belittled her every chance he got.

Each time over the years, when he sensed she was ready to leave him, he would threaten her family, thinking that by staying, she was saving them. But now, she had two children who only had her to protect them. They needed her alive and healthy.

"Our plane leaves at 3:00." She had never before dared to lie to him, but today she was able to do so with a sincere look on her face.

"Okay, I'll be home about 1:00 to drive you to the airport. By the way, Willow, I won't allow you to take any of the clothes you bought with my money," and he walked out the door

As soon as she saw him drive away, she called the non-emergency police number. Since giving birth to Antonio, she had purchased three new outfits. She already had one of them on for the trip. If she couldn't take them, she would have nothing to wear that fit her. She wasn't overweight at all, but she still had a little baby fat.

The police department answered on the first ring. "Hello, I have a question," Willow explained, "My children and I are packing to leave my husband and fly back to South Dakota to family. He says I can't take any of the clothes I bought with his money. Can he really stop me from packing those items?

"No ma'am, your clothes are your clothes, no matter whose money paid for them. After looking at your address, I see that we had officers at that address last evening. If you want, we'll be happy to send a couple of officers out to be present in the house while you pack. They can stay until you leave."

"Thank you," Willow replied, "I don't think that will be necessary. He offered to come home and drive us to the airport. But my plan is to already be at the airport before that happens. I wouldn't feel safe in a vehicle with him."

Willow was glad that Brenda was next door and could see Frank leave. Brenda drove over to Willow's house shortly after he left. She was early but she would help Willow with the kids while she packed. Plus, Brenda wanted to get them all out of there before Frank came back as much as Willow did.

Willow quickly dug four suitcases out of the closet. One would have to be filled with Antonio's cloth diapers. Disposable diapers were on the market but Willow knew she would not be able to afford them for a long while.

One suitcase held Anna Maria's clothes and some of her small toys. The third and fourth bags held Tony's and Willow's things. She couldn't take everything but this would get them by for a while.

The suitcases were closed up and Brenda began to load them into her trunk. She came back into the house with a question.

"What are you planning for your winter jackets and boots and things?"

"We'll just have to leave them. There's no way I'll be able to manage all that on the plane." Willow sighed.

"I have an idea. I'll take them to my house and box it all up and mail it to you later. How about that?"

"That would be so wonderful if you would do that, but it will take a lot of postage and I don't know when I can pay you back. We'll just leave them."

"It'll be my gift. You don't have to pay me back. Go get them and I'll run them home now and be right back."

Thank you so much. That is so wonderful of you, my friend," Willow touched her arm as she expressed her deep gratitude. It would save her a lot of money when winter came to South Dakota.

Chapter 11

As they drove to the airport, Willow remained anxious. She constantly was looking behind them, fearing she'd see Frank following them.

With plenty of time to spare, they arrived at the airport. Brenda helped get them out of the car and she stayed with them until they located their tickets. The four suitcases were checked in and taken away by the baggage handlers.

Brenda said her teary good-byes, wished them well and couldn't help but pull out a Kleenex as she walked away. She wished she could have done more to help Willow who had become a dear friend. She would miss her but she would pray for all three of them.

Willow entered the waiting area for passenger boarding carrying her purse and Antonio's diaper bag over her left shoulder. He was in her left arm, and Anna's little fingers were wrapped tightly around two fingers on Willow's right hand.

Locating a bench that had room for all of them to sit, she sat down and organized her diaper bag to make everything easily accessible once they boarded the plane. She carried two bottles for Antonio just in case of any delays.

As she looked around the room she noticed a large police presence. It wasn't a large airport but as her eyes searched the area, she counted six uniformed officers. Two of them were watching her and the children and the others were watching the entrances and exits to that area. She silently thanked God for their presence. The only things she knew Frank to be afraid of were the police and going to jail.

Perhaps the police department had finally taken her seriously after her call about him not letting her take her clothes. The officers who came to their house the night before certainly hadn't done so.

Time passed quickly as they waited for their flight to be announced. On the plane, Anna Maria had her own seat and Willow would hold Antonio. The plane wasn't quite full and Willow sighed as she again thanked God. She was relieved that the third seat in their row was empty. Anna wanted to be touching her mother, if she couldn't be on her lap. Willow understood her need.

Once airborne, Willow knew they were finally safe. She could breathe a little easier. After surviving the initial ear plugging time, both children seemed to sense it was okay and began to relax.

Willow was smack in the middle of a miracle and she smiled as she mouthed *Thank you Lord.* Her mind flashed back to the first time he hit her. It was years ago. If she had left him then, she could have avoided the last few years of bruises and heartache. But had she left then, she wouldn't have her children who she loved more than anything. She desired a normal family life for them. But it wasn't to be.

She couldn't have foreseen the future back then. But she wished she hadn't been so naïve. There were so many warning signs and she missed them all. Or maybe she was willfully blind to them all.

She thought he loved her. She wanted to believe he loved her, but he loved that he could control her. He was good at that by keeping her without a job, without a car, without friends and without her family. She thought he would change but he never did. He had come too close to killing her this time.

Now she would look ahead and work hard to make a new life for the kids and herself in the safe community of her family. For now she knew her sister's home was going to be a safe place for them to be. She was on an airplane going to safety with her two kids, three dollars and four suitcases.

That morning before she told Frank they were leaving, he looked at her saying he was sorry, in his most sincere, teary-eyed look. Even when she looked straight into his eyes, she wasn't moved whatsoever. Her heart was forever dead to his charisma, his charm, and his supposed love. He had destroyed it all last night when he nearly killed her.

When the plane landed, Willow waited for the passengers behind them to get their carry-ons and walk past them. With both seat belts undone, she stood and once again put her purse and little Tony's diaper bag, now down to one bottle, over her left shoulder. Tony in her left arm and Anna Maria's hand wrapped around her fingers on her right hand they left the plane.

They made their way to the area where those meeting passengers waited. She spotted Lindy and the boys. Her chin quivered and tears began to flow. She had to concentrate on getting her emotions in check. She didn't want Anna Maria to see her mom crying. Anna had been traumatized enough and she didn't want to add to it.

Lindy was close enough to them to see Willow fighting tears. That was enough to get her started. But, by the time they were close enough for hugs, both sisters had regained control of their emotions. Unspoken was *remain stoic for the kids.* The boys and Lindy were able to get all the bags as the luggage appeared.

Chapter

12

Once in the car, Lindy explained that the reason Lyle hadn't come along, was to make sure there would be plenty of room in the car. Lindy thought having the boys along might offer a distraction, at least for Anna Maria, but she wouldn't leave her mothers side even for two seconds. So both kids and Willow all joined Lindy in the driver's seat sat in the front seat with Lindy. The boys sat in the back seat.

Lyle would have supper ready for them when they arrived at the farm. He was a great cook but for tonight he made a kid-friendly meal of sloppy joes, pork and beans and French fries. For dessert he planned chocolate ice cream.

Willow was able to quietly let Lindy know not to talk about last night until after she put Anna Maria to bed. She was not quite three and had survived a terrifying event. She watched her father nearly kill her mother.

Lindy suggested that she and Willow clean up the kitchen, and Lyle and the boys could show Anna some of the boys toys and stuffed animals but they changed that plan when they saw the fear on Anna's face. She wanted to stay where she could see her mother.

So Willow had Anna sit in a large wrap-around chair beside Tony and asked her to try to help Tony sit upright. Both kids were satisfied while the moms finished the dishes.

Lindy held Antonio while Willow went to the bedroom with Anna in tow, to the room they'd be sleeping in. They emerged with pajamas for both kids. Willow took him while she put his jammies on and then gave him back to Linden to hold while she got Anna into hers.

Willow held Anna Maria tightly while she rocked her to sleep. She knew the little girl had to be tired and she went quickly to sleep. So did Antonio, in Lindy's arms. They laid them both in the bed where the three of them would be sleeping while they were there. They assembled a pillow barrier next to Antonio, so he wouldn't roll off.

~

Lindy reached for the wine glasses and poured them each a glass. She stopped at the boys' room to see if Lyle wanted to join them in the living room.

"You were a huge part of our miracle by wiring the money for the tickets. I don't know when I can repay you, but I will," Willow told Lindy.

"Well, let me tell you about that," Lindy began. "I've never wired money before. First I wondered who in town could actually wire money at all. I hoped a travel agent could do so. The only one in town is Jorgenson's Travel. I wasn't sure they were even open on Saturday but I hoped and I prayed they were.

When I dialed, the phone rang and rang and rang. I closed my eyes and said, "Please God! Let someone be there. I don't think I have any other options." I was just ready to hang up when suddenly Jack Jorgensen said, "Hello!" rather gruffly.

After I explained what I needed, and that it was for you, he assured me he could handle it. Then he told me they aren't ever open on Saturdays.

He said, "I was working on a file for a customer at home and realized I had left some needed papers at the office. I just drove in to the office to pick them up and planned to turn right around and go home.

He said, "I wasn't going to answer the phone. I was standing by the door to leave, but something, maybe God, said pick up the phone." The urging wouldn't leave so finally I did pick up.

Lindy was so relieved. Jorgenson knew the family and he remembered Willow from high school. He was happy to be able to make arrangements for the tickets and help Willow get home.

A few minutes later he called Lindy to tell her it was all taken care of. Following that phone call, Lindy called Willow to give her the good word that the tickets were at the airport for her. Willow could pick them up at the airline counter when she arrived at the airport.

As Willow listened to Lindy tell that story, she was shocked. Her eyes began to get watery. So many things had come together perfectly for the three of them to safely escape from Frank. Now she was sitting here safely in Lindy and Lyle's living room with a glass of wine. She looked to heaven and thanked God. She had truly felt God's presence ever since the night before. He had calmed her spirit and given her a plan. She felt sure that He would take care of getting them safely away.

When Lyle joined them Willow relayed the entire event to them. They were both surprised to see that even though it was twenty-four hours later, she still had the clear marks his fingers had left on her neck. Lindy's mouth opened as she realized how close they came to losing Willow just the night before.

They were both so thankful they had been able to help her get to safety. They hoped that Frank would leave her alone now so she could find a job, a place to live and begin a new life for the children and for herself.

Lindy was sure their parents would be willing to help Willow rent a house or apartment and maybe buy her a used car to give her a chance to be on her own. They hadn't mentioned Willow's coming to her parents or any other family member because they wanted to get her home safely first before letting anyone know. There would be plenty of time for that later.

Chapter 13

Several days after they arrived in Watertown, Anna Maria began to vomit violently. It continued through the day and seemed to be even worse the following day.

They made an appointment for her with Dr. Edwards, Lindy's family doctor. A pediatrician would have been an hour away. The doctor was somewhat aware of them just arriving to Watertown. He did understand that Willow had no insurance, but Lindy promised to pay the bill for Anna's visit.

The tests they did on little Anna Maria revealed that she was dehydrated but nothing else. No virus or infection. "After doing the blood tests, I'm hoping it's just a twenty four hour bug. But if she's not a lot better tomorrow, I want to see her again. We don't want her to get any more dehydrated. Try to encourage as many liquids as she'll take. We won't make an appointment. If she is still vomiting just bring her in."

Anna was still vomiting the next day with no sign of it

letting up. They called to alert Dr. Edward's office that they were returning to his office.

Lindy drove so Willow could tend to Anna Maria as they drove to the clinic. Lyle had plenty of farm work to do, but was happy to stay with Antonio while they took Anna to the doctor. He knew Willow would need Lindy's help on the way.

Dr. Edwards was alarmed at Anna Maria's deteriorating condition. They would have to act quickly.

"I'm sending her to Children's Hospital in Sioux Falls. I will call and alert them that she's coming. We can send her by ambulance or if you can leave right away, you can take her by car. It's about an hour to Children's Hospital.

Going by car would be less frightening for her than an ambulance. If Lindy is with you, she can drive so you can hold Anna."

"Yes, she drove me here today. She's in the waiting room. Can you come out and give her the directions to Children's hospital?"

"Certainly," Dr. Edwards said. He followed them out to the waiting room and proceeded to explain the necessity of the urgent trip and the directions to the hospital.

Lindy asked if she could use the phone at the receptionist's desk to call home. "Lyle, we need to hurry and get Anna to Children's hospital in Sioux Falls. Will you call Marigold to see if she can come and stay with Antonio? If she can, you can get back out into the field. We may be at the hospital awhile."

"Oh my goodness! Yes, I will see if she can come out. But I may hang around in here until you get there. Call and let me know what they say. I'll say a prayer right now."

"Good idea, Lyle. I think she is going to need lots of prayers. You maybe should call Mom and Dad after you call Mari. They'll all pray. Lyle, Dr. Edwards is very concerned about Anna." Lindy's voice cracked.

"Drive carefully, Lindy. Take a deep breath. Willow will need your strength so she can be strong. I love you, Lind" Lyle ended the call and immediately said a prayer for their safe trip and for Anna's life.

In the car, Anna Maria's little body was listless in her mother's arms. From time to time her little body trembled. It seemed to them she was lapsing into unconsciousness.

"My Father in Heaven," Willow began, "I need you so much right now. I'm so afraid for Anna Maria. I know you have known her and loved her since before she was born.

She needs you to help her right now. I'm her mother and I should know how to help her, but I don't. Please help the doctors find out what is wrong. Don't take her from me, Lord. I couldn't bear it." She wiped away her tears

Neither Willow nor Lindy talked much on the way. They were both frightened to see how quickly Anna's condition appeared to be deteriorating. They were both praying silently.

There wasn't much traffic and Lindy was able to speed a little. If she were to be stopped, she would ask the officer to give them an escort to the hospital.

Finally they were at the hospital. Lindy pulled into the emergency entrance as Dr. Edwards had advised her. There they were met with a doctor and two nurses. One of the nurses held out her arms to take Anna Maria's limp body. That nurse and the doctor quickly walked into the hospital. The other nurse explained to Willow and Linden that they would immediately get her started on an IV and go from there.

Linden went to park the car and Willow was advised to go to the admissions office to fill out paperwork. There she was presented with forms inquiring as to how she would pay for this. Willow wanted to cry. She needed to get to Anna's side, but she knew she had to be honest to this woman about her financial situation.

"We just arrived here a few days ago. We escaped from my husband. I don't have insurance. I don't have any money. I don't even have a job yet. I hope you can still help my daughter."

"Mrs. Rossi, this hospital does have a program that helps with people who are in your situation. The group that hands out financial grants is meeting tomorrow. I can't promise, of course, but I'm very sure that they will find your case eligible.

For now I will tell you that you have enough to worry about with the health of your daughter. You will get a written notice in the mail of their decision. I'll get someone to guide you to where she is. It was nice to meet you, Mrs. Rossi."

With that, the admissions desk worker called a volunteer to help Willow get back to where they were treating Anna. Willow was humbled. She had never run into people who were so nice in Kansas

Anna Maria was awake and looked terrified. When she saw Willow she cried "Mommy!" and held out her hands to Willow. Because of the IV to which Anna was hooked up, Willow couldn't completely grasp her into her comforting arms but she leaned over Anna and soothed and comforted her as much as she could.

"The doctors are working to help you to feel better honey," she explained. "Mommy will stay with you now. Don't worry." The doctors and the nurses will be very gentle and kind. When Anna Maria noticed Willow was smiling, relaxed and having pleasant conversations with them, she relaxed some.

Anna Maria would be held at least over night so Lindy said her goodbyes. She made sure Willow was fine sleeping in a chair in Anna's room for overnight. Lindy would go home to her family.

Marigold had been at the farm since lunchtime watching Antonio. He was a good baby at four months old, but he was a little nervous with the tension in the house. He knew his mom and his older sister were not there.

Marigold was happy that little Tony had napped most of the afternoon. Lyle had gone out to the field after Lindy called to report they had arrived at the hospital. He had been watching for Lindy's car to come down the road. When he saw her arrive, he finished what he was doing and called it a day.

He knew this had been a stressful day for Lindy and wanted to be there for her. He also wanted to hear about what happened at the hospital and how Willow and Anna Maria were holding up. He had been praying while he was in the field.

Back at the hospital, a variety of tests had been conducted on Anna since she had arrived the day before. They were finding nothing that would explain the reason for her extreme dehydration. They wanted her to stay one more day for psychological tests. Willow called Lindy to let her know.

Just before supper Willow called Lindy again. She wanted to talk to Antonio. By now she knew he would be really missing her. She also wanted to bring them up to date with Anna.

"You should see how big he smiled when he heard your voice, Willow. He's doing just fine. The boys have been playing with him non-stop since they got home from school. They love to make him giggle. He'll be very happy to see both of you, but he's doing extremely well. My boys have fallen in love with little Antonio. I'm so thankful you are all here with us so the boys can get to know each other."

"Yes, it's been a good cousin bonding time. Lindy, what would I ever do without you? I love you so much, you dear sister." Willow said tearing up.

"Love you too, Willow, and we love both Antonio and Anna Maria. What is the latest with her? Can she be released tomorrow?"

"Well, yes. Today she has spent time with a pediatric psychiatrist. They honestly cannot find any physical reason for her to be sick. She has good color and the light is back in her eyes. And she's eating well." Willow reported.

"But listen to this, Lindy, her psychiatrist asked me if we had been talking about the trauma of the night we left Frank? Or talked about him much since."

"And we haven't, wasn't that the right way to do it?" Lindy asked.

"I guess not. We have been wrong to avoid discussing Frank in front of her. Anna Maria's psychiatrist and psychologist both agree that Anna is a very bright and sensitive child. Yet, at three years old, its impossible for her to formulate the grown up questions she has. With us avoiding discussing him, she is not getting any answers to her questions. All of her ongoing curiosity together with her traumatic memories of the night of our escape is creating a physical reaction from her little body. She needs to know that Frank isn't coming here and that we're all safe."

"Oh, Willow, I'm so sorry. But how were we to know?"

"None of us knew. I was sure we were doing the best thing. I'm so sorry that we kept it all from her. Thinking about it now makes sense to me. Doesn't it to you?"

"Yes, it sure does. Did they say when she'll be released?" Asked Lindy?

"If nothing changes overnight, she can leave here tomorrow, whenever you can come get us. The hospital has done all they can for her. We'll leave with a prescription for her and they have already made a follow up appointment with a doctor in Watertown. They'll send her records to Watertown.

"By the way, I'll be very glad to get to your house and get a shower.

"They have given me some reading homework that I'll share with you and Lyle. We'll explain it to your boys, too, instead of keeping things from her, we'll talk about a few things from the past and also about our future plans.

"The doctors said that she has no way to know if she's safe here or if Antonio or I are safe. If she thinks I'm in any danger that puts her into a terrible emotional situation. If we don't discuss it with her, she has no way to feel secure. But they expect her to get over this and lead a very normal happy life."

"I'm so glad. It's interesting, isn't it? I'll follow your lead in the car tomorrow and after we get home. We'll do our best to make her feel safe and secure and that you all are in no danger." Lindy replied.

~

Linden and Lyle both came to pick up Willow and Anna Maria from the hospital. Along with them was little Antonio. Marigold agreed to pick up her son early from school and go to their house, to stay with their boys if they weren't home from the hospital yet, when the boys were due home from school. She also wanted to see Anna Maria and hug her as she welcomed her home

Anna Maria's eyes sparkled at the sight of her little brother. She cried a few tears of joy as she gave him a big hug. She was happy to see her aunt and uncle as well. With her mom's help, she soon had her jacket on and was ready to leave the hospital and get back to Lyle and Linden's farm.

Armed with their new information, conversation was more open in front of all the children. Anna Maria improved daily and Willow could once again, explore what jobs might be available to her.

Chapter

14

Willow's parents generously bought her a used, low mileage, Chevy van. Jason, Mari's husband, who was an exceptional auto mechanic, had checked it over and given his nod of approval that it was in excellent shape for being three years old. They wanted Willow and their grandchildren to be driving around town in a safe vehicle.

Willow was moved to tears at their generosity. Now she could make appointments for job interviews and not have to constantly be asking to borrow Lindy's car. Lindy had no problem watching her niece and nephew while Willow went to interviews. They were all cheering for and praying for her to find the perfect job.

Julie, a friend of Lindy's, taught third grade at the elementary school. She became aware that the school receptionist was leaving soon. The day Julie was assured that the receptionist had given her notice, she called Lindy, to have her relay that information to Willow, with instructions to get over there to apply for the job as soon as she could. It might even mean they wouldn't need to post the job opening to the public.

Lindy searched her closet for the perfect outfit for Willow to borrow to go into the school. She would just go in asking to fill out an application, but if everything worked out and the principal would be in his office, she might get an interview right away.

Watertown was a small town so everyone knew from the local gossip that Willow had returned to town, now as a single mom. In fact, Willow had accidently run into the principal's secretary in the grocery store the day before. Willow told her she was seriously looking for a job so she and the kids could stay in Watertown.

She remembered Willow from high school and knew what a bright woman she was, and knew her parents and sisters well. She invited Willow to come to the school to ask for an application and said she would put in a good word for her to the principal.

Willow was hired that day. This was indeed the perfect job. To make it even better, the school had recently opened an onsite day care for teachers and other staff. Willow would not have to drop the kids off at a stranger's house before work. She could take them with her to work. She could even visit them on her lunch break.

She was ecstatic. That would help so much with Anna's insecurities. When they were old enough to start school, they would have the same vacations and days off. Willow thanked God. He had been so good.

If she were very careful with her money, she would be able to afford a two-bedroom apartment. She didn't need to buy a car now because of her parent's generosity. But they all needed clothing and they had no furniture.

Between her family and their friends, most knew Willow and loved her. Soon they had furnished her apartment with second hand furniture, at least with the basics. Her sisters had friends whose children had outgrown some clothing and before she knew it, the kids both had plenty of clothes with more promised as the seasons changed

Marigold gave Willow a generous gift certificate to the local ladies-wear store so she could get herself some professional clothing. She wanted to help. She knew that Lindy and Lyle had been feeding them and housing them plus all the trips to Sioux Falls. She and Jason could afford the gift and she wanted to help in a meaningful way.

Things fell together quickly. The family of three moved into their apartment and Willow, with the help of her family, decorated the apartment to be cozy and homey.

The two children were sharing a room. Antonio quickly learned how to climb out of his crib, with some help from his sister. He would then crawl into bed with Anna Maria. She was a loving and protective big sister. Willow knew they both found security in being together.

Willow's new job and the new day care experience were both started without any problem. Within a few days life seemed to be settling into a routine. With the help of her family and friends, Willow was optimistic about a normal life. Her father and mother had separately given her a wad of cash for groceries or whatever, with the strict instructions not to mention it to anyone, especially their spouse.

They were fine. They were better than fine. Willow thanked

God for her many blessings. He had really taken care of her in so many ways. She asked him to let her know how she could give back and help someone who needed her.

~

Willow soon learned of a newly formed group for battered women and children that had recently been formed in Watertown. She volunteered as a mentor to the women who needed encouragement to leave their husband or boyfriend. She helped them to understand that the abuse would never stop and the degree of violence would continually grow.

The thing she stressed the most was, now that they were out in one piece, they must never ever to go back. Many did go back and some were beaten to death.

She was involved with many fundraisers until they could discontinue using hotel rooms and buy a safe house for the women and children. It was her way of giving back. It made her time with Frank worth something so she didn't feel like the years were wasted.

She let it be known at the school about her mentorship job with battered women. She was able to refer teachers and even moms of students to a place where they could receive help.

The safe house became a reality just one year later. It was an older large home in a quiet residential neighborhood. It had six bedrooms and a large storage room that could be made into an extra bedroom if needed. They hired twenty-four hour security and everyone who worked there was given a background test and sworn to secrecy about where the house was located.

In just a few months the house was filled with mothers and children who had escaped their homes, oftentimes in their pajamas. Further fundraisers were held to buy clothing and personal items for the women and their children. The entire community and several small towns around Watertown were more supportive at making meaningful donations than they could have hoped. There was big need everywhere!

They were able to get local doctors, psychologists and social workers to volunteer their time to patch up the women and children as needed. There were obvious physical and emotional needs on an ongoing basis. Most often, self-confidence and self-worth were the hardest things for these women to learn.

In time they were able to get counselors to help the women find good jobs. If necessary they would find jobs in another city away from their abuser, but always with a mentor close by to help keep them safe. It took a lot of counseling and caring to help the women overcome the sense of worthlessness with which they had been living.

Willow was content to be a big supporter of the house but never wanted to be involved full time. She had compassion for the women and children but she didn't want her children involved with that life of strife and chaos.

It took several months but Anna Maria was becoming a happy little girl who knew she was well loved and protected by her grandma and grandpa and her aunts and uncles and cousins. Her little brother, Antonio was a handsome and bright toddler. His complexion matched Anna Maria's olive skin and dark hair and dark eyes. Both children loved their mother deeply and if there was anything they knew for sure it was that Jesus loved them and so did their mommy.

The End!

About the Author

Carol Farris is retired and lives in Nebraska where both her children, along with their families also reside. This is her first published book but will be the first in a series. Even though it took her until the age of seventy-six to finish her book, she reminds us that if God wants something to happen, it will eventually happen.

Thank you for reading

Two Kids, Three Dollars, and Four Suitcases.

By Carol Farris

Look for my next book about Willow, and how she discovered the way to find perfect peace in the midst of chaos. *The peace that passes all understanding. She'll share the secret.*

This book is written for women of any age who discover they are involved or about to be involved in a relationship that may have started to be a loving one. Yet something in the gut yells the message, "*proceed with extreme caution.*"

Instead of deep and unfailing love, you could be headed for heartache, betrayal, and physical as well as psychological abuse. Rarely is there physical abuse that isn't also accompanied by extreme control causing emotional and psychological abuse.

Guard your heart girl!

Grow stronger in your weakness!

2 Corinthians 12:9-10

But he said to me, " My grace is sufficient for you, for ***my power is made perfect in weakness.*** *Therefore I will boast all the more gladly about my weaknesses, so that Christ's power may rest on me.*

That is why for Christ's sake I delight in weaknesses, in insults, in hardships, imperfections, in difficulties.

For when I am weak, then I am strong

Know two things absolutely for sure…

-The first is that God's timing is always perfect!

He never seems to be in a hurry, but know that He is always working in the background for you.

-And secondly, that we are to be thankful for Adversity!

Always give thanks, no matter what…

PGIL2020USA